SHE WAS ALREADY IN HIS BED, WAITING FOR HIM ...

"You're late," Deirdre said.

"I know. I had something to do first," he said, undressing.

"You know, you must be the most infuriating man I've ever met. I don't know why I come here, why I let you do the things you do to me."

"Because you love them," he said, sliding into the bed and touching her bare shoulder. He gathered her up into his arms and she was powerless to stop him — physically, or emotionally. Eagerly she pressed her body against him.

"Damn you, Tracker," she said as she matched the rhythm of his hips. "Damn you, damn you, damn you..."

Avon Books are available at special quantity discounts for
bulk purchases for sales promotions, premiums, fund
raising or educational use. Special books, or book excerpts,
can also be created to fit specific needs.

For details write or telephone the office of the Director of
Special Markets, Avon Books, Dept. FP, 1790 Broadway,
New York, New York 10019, 212-399-1357.

TOM CUTTER

TRACKER 3

THE BLUE CUT JOB

AVON
PUBLISHERS OF BARD, CAMELOT, DISCUS AND FLARE BOOKS

THE BLUE CUT JOB is an original publication of Avon
Books. This work has never before appeared in book form.

AVON BOOKS
A division of
The Hearst Corporation
1790 Broadway
New York, New York 10019

Copyright © 1983 by Robert J. Randisi
Published by arrangement with the author
Library of Congress Catalog Card Number: 83-90794
ISBN: 0-380-84483-4

First Avon Printing September, 1983

AVON TRADEMARK REG. U. S. PAT. OFF. AND IN
OTHER COUNTRIES, MARCA REGISTRADA, HECHO EN U. S. A.

Printed in the U. S. A.

WFH   10 9 8 7 6 5 4 3 2 1

For Anna and Christopher

Part One

[Prologue]

September 6, 1881

As the Chicago & Alton train passed through the region of Glendale, Missouri, conductor Hazelback never considered the possibility that his train might be robbed. Not when, only a scant two months before, the Chicago, Rock Island & Pacific train had already been robbed, and one man—a conductor—had been killed. No, thought Hazelback, no one in his right mind would pull a second job so close to a first.

So naturally, as the train was brought to a stop in a deep ravine known as Blue Cut, Hazelback assumed that there was some engine difficulty.

The engineer, however, whose name was Foote, knew differently. He had stopped the train because ahead of him on the tracks was a pile of stones with a red flag sitting atop it, and behind that stood a man with his arms folded across his chest. In almost the next instant, the engine was boarded and Foote and his fireman, John Steading, were ordered to get out. Once on the ground Foote could see that about a dozen men in all were proceeding to board every car in the train.

The man who had been standing on the tracks was apparently the leader of the gang, and as he approached, Foote could see that he was wearing a white sack over his head with eye holes cut out so that he could see.

"Let's go," he told Foote, giving him a push. Together they walked back to the express car, which was locked.

Cursing, the leader asked Foote, "What's the express man's name?"

"F-Fox," the engineer answered.

Since the door was locked from the outside, it was obvious that Fox had jumped off the train and hidden.

"Call out to Mr. Fox," the leader told Foote, "and tell him that if he does not come up here with the key, I shall surely shoot you dead."

To illustrate his point, the robber placed the barrel of his gun against the frightened engineer's head.

"Fox!" the engineer called out. "For God's sake, man, he'll kill me if you don't come out with the key!"

When the man did not appear, the robber leader cocked the hammer on his revolver, and Foote shouted in anguish, "Fox!"

In a matter of seconds Fox appeared from the brush alongside the tracks and approached them. The hooded leader put his hand out for the key, and when Fox handed it to him, clubbed him with his gun. Fox fell to the ground, bleeding and unconscious.

"Open it," the leader said, tossing the key to one of his men, whose head was also covered by a hood.

The man opened the door and entered the car. A few moments later he reappeared holding a canvas money sack.

"How much?" the leader asked.

"Only twenty-five hundred," the man answered, and the leader cursed so angrily that the engineer was sure he was as good as dead.

"Let's see what the passengers have," the leader said. He pushed the engineer and directed a third bandit, "Take him back to his place."

Conductor Hazelback had barely enough time to tell the passengers to hide their valuables before the car was entered by four men. The group's leader cursed and ranted as his men derived precious little booty from the passengers. He decided that they had hidden their most valuable goods.

For this he seemed to blame the conductor, Hazelback. He pushed his gun into the man's face and said,

"Smell that, damn you! This pistol has already killed one conductor."

It was then that Hazelback realized these were the same men who had robbed the Chicago, Rock Island & Pacific train in July, when a conductor named Westfall had been killed.

"All of you," the man shouted now. "Are your valuables precious enough to die for?"

One by one the people began to produce their valuables. None was willing to die for them. Up toward the front of the car there seemed to be some trouble. The leader walked forward and asked, "What the hell is going on?"

"This gentleman doesn't seem to want us to take his watch," one of his men answered.

The gentleman in question was a large man in his late thirties, well dressed with a neatly trimmed beard.

"Please," the man said, addressing himself to the leader, "it was a gift from someone very special—"

The man was holding the watch in his right hand and the leader reached out and snatched it from him. The watch was gold and rather large.

"Does it keep good time?" he asked.

"Perfect," the well-dressed man assured him.

"That's a shame," the leader said, pocketing the watch. "If you had said no, I'd have let you keep it."

"Please, mister—" the man began, rising a bit.

"If he says another word, kill him," the leader instructed his men. Upon hearing that, the well-dressed man sank back into his seat, raging silently.

The robber leader did not know what he had!

Now that the passengers had produced their goods, the haul began to look better, what with jewelry and cash, but the leader was still angry about the small amount of money they had gotten from the express car. He walked back to the conductor and put his gun under his nose again.

"You tell your employers that the next time a reward is offered for the James gang, we'll burn their damned trains. You got that? Tell your bosses and that damned governor of Missouri. One more reward!"

And with that the hooded men vanished from the train. It took some time before anyone had the nerve

11

to step out of the train, but when they did they found that all the bandits were gone. Hazelback checked with engineer Foote. They found that no one had been killed, and the only person injured had been the express man, Fox.

"This is amazing," Foote said to Hazelback. "What kind of men would rob another train so soon after the last one? Madmen!"

"Did you see the leader?" Hazelback asked. "He admitted to me that he shot Westfall. By God, Foote, this was the James gang, and that man was Jesse James!"

[1]

March 9, 1882

The man who entered the lobby of the Farrell House hotel was a heavyset man, not tall but large, impeccably dressed with a neatly trimmed beard and hair. He also carried himself like a man used to having people step aside for him. His pace never slackened as he approached the front desk.

"Good morning, sir," the red-haired girl standing behind the desk greeted him politely. Her name was Shana Sullivan, and working behind the front desk was something new to her. Her brother Will had worked for some time as a bartender in the adjoining saloon, but this was her first week behind the desk, and it still felt strange to her.

"Polite" was the key word to working behind the desk, though, and she always kept that in mind. The people on the other side of the desk did *not* always have that in mind, however, and this man was such a case.

"I want to talk to Tracker," he said curtly.

Shana had been briefed on how to handle such requests.

"Would you like a room, sir?" she asked.

"If I wanted a room, I would have asked for one," the man replied rudely. "I want to talk to Tracker, and that's all that I want."

"If you are not staying here, where are you staying?" Shana asked.

Shana was aware that she should have included the word "sir" somewhere in that sentence, but the man was getting her Irish up. When that happened, she didn't necessarily do what she was supposed to.

"Look, lady—" the man began.

At that point Duke Farrell, who had been standing to the side listening, stepped forward. He was the "Farrell" for which the hotel was named, but he did not own any part of it. If Farrell's role had to be defined, he would probably be called the manager of the hotel—though he was much more than that.

"Is there a problem, Shana?" he asked.

"This young...lady doesn't have a problem," the man said, not giving Shana a chance to answer. "I am the one who has a problem."

"Oh?" Farrell asked, crossing his arms across his chest. Shana's anger was fading, mainly because of how funny the two men looked as they faced each other. Duke Farrell was barely five and a half feet tall and he weighed considerably less than the large man he was facing. The tableau they presented, standing there facing each other, was nothing but funny.

"Are you a guest in the hotel?" Duke asked. "Or are you thinking about becoming a guest?"

"A hotel room is the least of my problems, damn it!" the man exploded. "I have to see Tracker."

"Mr. Tracker *is* a guest in the hotel," Duke continued, "so you can see that I would be more concerned about his problems than I would be about yours."

"What does that mean?"

"That means that everyone who comes in here to see Mr. Tracker is not just given his room number," Duke explained. "If you will tell Miss Sullivan where you are staying, we will give the information to Mr. Tracker, and then he'll contact you."

"I don't have time—"

"I think you'll have to make time," Duke told him, cutting the man off. "Give Shana your name, tell her where you're staying and what the nature of your business is. All of that information will be given to Tracker," Duke finished up, with a look on his face that said, "That's it." Then he turned on his heel and walked away.

The large man stood there mutely staring at Farrell's retreating back. Then he turned to Shana, who gave him her best smile and prepared to write down whatever the man told her.

[2]

"Okay, so what's his name and what's his business?" Tracker asked Duke.

A few hours had passed, and Duke had finally been able to trace Tracker to a poker game. He allowed Tracker to finish the hand he was involved with, then drew him off to the side to talk to him.

Tracker and Duke were friends, but they were opposites both physically and psychologically. Duke was five and a half feet tall, while Tracker was six-four. Duke liked to talk, while Tracker preferred action. The friendship might have been odd, but while they were opposites, they also complemented one another. When Tracker had won the San Francisco hotel in a poker game, his natural choice for someone to run it had been Duke. Tracker lived there, but only a handful of people knew that he owned the place.

That is, half of it.

The other half was owned by a girl named Deirdre Long, who had inherited it from her father. Actually, Tracker owned fifty-one percent, so he had the final say in hotel matters. He rarely meddled, however, leaving hotel matters to Duke and Deirdre.

Now he and Duke were discussing a different kind of business.

Reading from Shana's notes, Duke said, "The guy's

name is William Duncan and he's staying at the Alhambra, in the square."

"The square" was Portsmouth Square, where most of the larger hotels and gambling houses were located. Farrell House was situated about a block off the square, and sometimes picked up some overflow business.

"Duncan," Tracker repeated. "I never heard of him. What's his business?"

Duke frowned at Shana's notes and said, "It looks like it says 'Blue Cut job.' That ring a bell?"

He looked at Tracker, who was staring off into space. "Tracker?"

"It sounds familiar," Tracker said, still gazing off, "but I can't put my finger on it." Tracker looked right at Duke and asked, "Is there anything else on there?"

Duke checked, then shrugged and said, "No, that's it."

"What did you think of the guy?"

"He was rude to Shana, pushy...but he looks like money, Tracker."

"How much money?"

Duke smiled and said, "A lot of money."

Tracker threw a glance over at the poker table, then shook his head and said, "Let me cash in, Duke, and we'll go over and check out Mr. Duncan."

[3]

Tracker waited outside the Alhambra while Duke went inside to talk to the desk clerk and manager of the hotel. They had only been in San Francisco a relatively short time, but Duke had a penchant for making "contacts." Now he was going to use some of them to get some information on Duncan.

After a short time he came out of the Alhambra and Tracker asked, "You find out anything?"

"A few things. Listen, you want to talk to this guy tonight, or do you want to go back to the hotel and discuss what I've found out?"

Gazing up at the upper floors of the Alhambra Hotel, Tracker scratched his neck absently and said, "Why don't we let him wait until tomorrow. Let's go back and have a couple of drinks."

"I'm for that."

They walked back to the Farrell House, but instead of going into the hotel they went into the adjoining saloon, which was part of the hotel. They went to the bar and ordered two beers from the bartender, Will Sullivan, Shana's brother.

When Tracker first met Will he was an over-the-hill prizefighter who thought he had one fight left. Once he got that out of his system, he was content to work in the saloon as a bartender. He, Shana, and Deirdre Long were the only other people who knew that Tracker actually owned the hotel and didn't just live in it.

"What are you fellas up to?" Will asked, setting their beers down on the bar.

"Just a friendly drink," Tracker said. "See you later, Will."

"Okay."

Duke was still the only one who knew exactly what Tracker did besides owning the hotel and playing poker. He was the only one who knew that "Tracker" was not just a name.

"Okay, so what's this 'Blue Cut job'?" Duke asked, as they took a corner table.

"I still haven't thought of it, but I will," Tracker said. "What did you find out at the Alhambra?"

"Duncan wired ahead for a reservation, and get this, he took the biggest suite they've got."

Tracker whistled and said, "Yeah, that's money, all right."

"Also, as soon as he got here he started asking about where he could find a man named Tracker. It seems all he was told was that you could be found in the Portsmouth Square area."

"Somebody must have given him my name," Tracker said. "Tomorrow I'll find out who."

Tracker had been very closemouthed about letting anyone know his whereabouts. He had, however, contacted a few people he relied on to refer work to him.

"So then tomorrow you're going to see this guy?" Duke asked.

"Oh, yes, I think so. I think I'd like to know very much what's on Mr. Duncan's mind."

"Without finding out what this Blue Cut job was?" Duke asked.

"Oh, I might remember that by tomorrow, but I don't think it matters all that much. I'm sure Mr. Duncan will refresh my memory for me."

"Where are you going to see him?" Duke asked.

"Oh, I think I'll send him a message to come here tomorrow, and I'll see him in *my* suite—although it's probably not as big as his."

"You want me to sit in on the meeting?"

19

Tracker stared at Duke until Duke started to become uncomfortable.

"No, Duke, I'll talk to the man alone."

"Okay, I just thought I'd ask."

"You asked."

"Is there anything you want me to do?" Duke asked.

"Yeah," Tracker said, "I think I'll let you deliver my message to Mr. Duncan. All right?"

"Sure, Tracker."

"Okay. We'll take care of that in the morning," Tracker said, rising.

"What are you going to do tonight? Another card game?"

"No, no card game," Tracker answered. "I've got another kind of game, and somebody to play it with waiting in my room."

"Deirdre," Duke said. He did not approve of Tracker juggling Deirdre and Shana, but Tracker freely admitted that he enjoyed both women, and could not choose between them.

Tonight it was Deirdre, tomorrow it would be Shana, the next night it could just as well be someone else.

That was the way Tracker was, though, and there wasn't much Duke could do about it. He just hoped that Deirdre wouldn't end up getting hurt.

"You better watch out that red-haired sister of Will's don't come up to your room while you're there with Deirdre," Duke warned.

"She knows better, Duke," Tracker said. "She knows a lot better."

[4]

Tracker actually passed Shana on his way upstairs and said good night. He marveled at how different two women could be. Shana knew that he slept with Deirdre as well as with her, and she didn't mind. On the other hand, Tracker wasn't sure of Deirdre. He had no way of knowing if she knew about Shana or not, but he'd never mention it to her.

Deirdre had traveled with her father for a long time before settling, and they had done their best to con people out of their hard-earned money. Her pa was one of the best con men around, and he taught her everything he knew. When they wound up with the hotel, they had decided to go straight and run it. Soon after that Deirdre's father died, and she ended up partners with one other man before that man lost his share to Tracker in a poker game.

Deirdre was independent and stubborn. She was also a good businesswoman. What she was not was a starry-eyed innocent. She had to know about Shana, but for some reason she would not mention it, and she would not let Shana and Tracker's relationship break up her own with Tracker.

Women were the oddest creatures—but they were also the loveliest.

And even in that the two women were so different. Shana was the taller of the two, and her hair was fiery red. She was full-breasted and uninhibited. Deirdre was blond and slender, with small but perfectly rounded breasts. When they were in bed she was responsive and loving, but she wouldn't do some of the things that Shana would. She would not experiment. There were times when Tracker did prefer one over the other, but in the long run it was not a decision he would like to make.

When he got to his room Deirdre was already in his bed, waiting.

"You're late," she told him.

"I know. I had something to do first," he said, undressing.

"You know, you must be the most infuriating man I've ever met. I don't know why I come here, why I let you do the things you do to me."

"Because you love them," he said, sliding onto the bed and touching her bare shoulder.

"I don't mean those things," she said, halfheartedly, pushing his hand away.

"We've had this conversation before," he said.

"I know, and it always ends the same way."

"And that's the way it's going to end now," he told her. He gathered her up into his arms and she was powerless—physically or emotionally—to stop him. As much as she liked to be in control, she could not be when she was with this man. She reacted to him as she had reacted to no other man in her life.

When he kissed her, all of her anger and frustration melted away, and her arms slid up around his neck. She pressed her body against his eagerly, feeling his pulsing manhood trapped between them. When his lips began to work on her, she wanted to speak but couldn't. When he worked his way down to her breasts and began to nibble on her nipples, she could only moan out loud.

At the same time, she loved and hated how helpless she felt when she was in his arms.

Gently—and he was almost always gentle with her— he pressed her down onto her back, mounted her, and slid himself deep inside of her. Then Tracker felt her arms glide up around him, and felt her nails dig into his back. He knew that there was a fire in her loins now that only he could quench, and he took his time doing so.

He kissed her again and her lips were feverish on his, her tongue alive inside his mouth. The scent of her was heavy in his nostrils, a scent all her own. He had never known two women who had the same scent when they were in bed. Maybe some of them wore the same perfume, but once in bed each had a scent of her own.

"Damn you, Tracker," she finally was able to say as she matched the rhythm of his hips. "Damn you, damn you, damn you..."

She was saying that because she didn't want him to hear what she really wanted to say. She didn't want to give him the satisfaction of hearing her say that she loved him.

She would never say that to him unless he said it to her first, and she knew that she had a long, long wait before that day would arrive.

So she loved him silently and damned him aloud, until the time came when she could no longer talk, but could only hold onto him while the whole world moved beneath them.

[5]

The following morning Deirdre stretched languidly as she watched Tracker dress, and asked, "What are you going to do this morning?"

"I'm going to go downstairs and have breakfast," he told her, "and then I'm going to come back up here for a business meeting."

She frowned and said, "What kind of a business meeting? You don't bother with hotel business."

Actually, that wasn't exactly true. Duke kept him up on all of the hotel business, but that was between him and Duke.

"This is not hotel business, Dee," he told her. "It's my kind of business."

"Oh," she said. She didn't know exactly what his kind of business was, but she knew it would be a hell of a lot more dangerous than hotel business. Tracker was the kind of man who couldn't live without danger.

"I guess you'll want me out of here before then," she remarked.

"I would appreciate it," he said, and then he walked over to her and ran one long finger over her right breast, stopping at the nipple, and added, "but that's only for the length of the meeting. I wouldn't want you to think I meant for you to stay out for good."

She looked at him in surprise, and felt a flutter in her stomach.

"That's probably the nicest thing you've ever said to me," she said.

He leaned over and kissed her gently and said, "Well, if that's true, it's my fault and not yours. I'll see you later."

He left the room feeling a little annoyed at himself, but then told himself that he shouldn't. Why shouldn't he say something nice to her once in a while? When they weren't in bed, they argued too much anyway. He should say nice things to her more often.

He'd have to work on that.

Downstairs Duke had already started breakfast. When the waiter saw Tracker enter the dining room, he knew what the big man would want for breakfast and went to inform the cook that it was time.

"You must have been hungry," Tracker said, seating himself across from Duke. Duke always sat so that when Tracker came he could sit facing the door, a prerequisite when you had the kind of past Tracker had. Tracker swore he would never let himself get caught with his back to his killer, the way Bill Hickok had.

"I just started."

The waiter brought Tracker a pot of coffee and he poured himself a cup.

"What's the message for Duncan?" Duke asked.

"Just tell him that I'd like to see him in my suite at the Farrell House."

"He'll pop his cork, since he was already here yesterday," Duke said.

"If it's important to him, he'll come."

"And if he doesn't?"

Tracker shrugged and said, "Then that'll mean it wasn't so important, won't it?"

"You're taking a chance on losing a lot of money, Tracker," Duke told him.

"If he came to San Francisco to see me, he'll see me. There's nobody else here who can do the job."

"What job?"

"Whatever the job is. If he needs me, then there are only a handful of other men who could do the job, and none of them are in San Francisco."

Interested, Duke asked, "Who are the other men?"

"Just some men who could do a job nearly as good as me," Tracker said.

"But not as good?"

"Nobody is as good at doing what I do, Duke, you know that," Tracker chided him.

"Name one man who is nearly as good as you."

Without thinking, Tracker replied, "Tal Roper."

"The Pinkerton man?"

"He used to be a Pinkerton, now he's out on his own," Tracker said. The waiter came and put his breakfast of steak and eggs in front of him. When he left, Tracker said, "Roper's a good man."

Tracker proceeded to eat his breakfast, and conversation fell to a minimum while both men finished.

"When do you want to see Duncan?" Duke asked while both were having their last cup of coffee.

"Right after you finish that cup, you can scoot over to the Alhambra and tell Mr. Duncan that I'll see him now."

Duke nodded, put down his empty cup and stood up. "You want us to check his gun when he goes up to see you?"

Tracker thought a moment, then said, "No, I don't think so. Just let him pass through. I'll tell Shana."

"All right. See you later."

Tracker knew it would take a while for Duke to walk over to the Alhambra, get to see Duncan, and give him the message, so he figured he had enough time for one more cup of coffee. After that, he went out to the desk to talk to Shana Sullivan.

"Morning, Shana," he greeted her.

"Good morning, Tracker," she said, obviously pleased to see him. "I notice that your Deirdre hasn't come down for breakfast yet," she commented.

"Maybe she's sleeping late," Tracker replied noncommittally. "I wish you two would let down your defenses and become friends."

"That's wishing for a lot," Shana told him. "What can I do for you today?"

"There'll be a man coming over to see me in a little while," he told her.

"That Duncan man from yesterday?" she asked, showing her distaste by distorting her beautiful face.

26

"Yeah, him," Tracker confirmed. "Try not to bite his head off and then let him come up and see me, okay?"

"Sure, I'll be sweet as pie—I'll pretend I'm Deirdre," she said, as if it were a wonderful idea that just dawned on her.

Tracker gave her a look that said, "Cut it out."

"Okay, okay, sorry," she said, putting her hands up in front of her. "I'll take care of it."

"Good. Thanks," he said, turning to go up the stairs to his room.

"Tracker?" she called.

"Yeah?" he said, turning back.

"Will we—uh—be seeing each other later?" she asked hopefully.

"Probably," he answered. "It will depend on what happens at this meeting."

She frowned and asked, "Are you . . . going away?"

He shrugged and repeated, "It will depend on what happens at this meeting. I'll let you know," he promised.

He went upstairs to his room to find Deirdre gone. She had made up the bed for him. He knew because if a maid had done it, she would have done a neater job.

There was a knock on the door and he figured it was too early for it to be Duncan, so it had to be Duke.

"Yeah, come on in."

Duke came in carrying a full bottle of bourbon and a couple of glasses.

"You deliver the message?" Tracker asked.

"Well, these aren't for you and me," Duke said, jiggling the hand that was holding the two glasses. "He said he'd be over as soon as he got dressed."

"What was his attitude?"

Duke put down the bottle and the glasses and said, "Better than yesterday. In fact, today he was even polite. Still pushy, but polite."

"Okay. Why don't you go and do whatever it is you do around here, and thanks for the bourbon."

"Sure. I'm going." Duke knew that Tracker liked to keep his business to himself, but he also knew that when the big man needed someone to bounce things off of, he came to good old Duke. "I'll talk to you later."

"Right."

When Duke left, Tracker thought that maybe he had

been too abrupt with him, but he didn't want Duke to think that, just because they were sort of partners in the hotel, they were partners in everything.

There was another knock on the door, this one harder, more formal than Duke's, so Tracker walked to the door and opened it. He recognized the man from Duke's description.

"Mr. Duncan?"

"Yes, William Duncan. And you are Mr. Tracker, I presume?" the man replied.

"That's right."

The two men studied each other for a few moments, and then Duncan stuck out his hand and they shook hands.

"Come on in," Tracker said, backing away to allow the other man room to enter. He closed the door after him and said, "Can I get you a drink? I've got some bourbon."

"Fine, that's fine."

Tracker studied the man as he poured two drinks, and he felt that here was a man ready to explode but trying to control himself. He walked across the room, handed him his drink, and said, "Why don't we get down to business before you bust."

Duncan took the drink and said, "Thanks. I'm in need of a man of your particular talents, and I'm willing to pay you very well."

"Wait a minute," Tracker said. "Which talents are you referring to?"

"Uh—" Duncan began, obviously a little confused, "I guess I need your talents as...a manhunter. Is that the proper term?"

"No, it's not," Tracker said.

"I understood you were a—uh—bounty hunter. Isn't that—"

"I used to be a bounty hunter, yes, Mr. Duncan, but I'm not anymore. If that's what you had in mind, then I guess we're both wasting—"

"No, wait. Wait a minute," Duncan interrupted. "I'm sorry if I've offended you. I've obviously been misinformed."

"By whom?"

"What?"

"Who did you get my name from?" Tracker asked.

Duncan hesitated, then said, "You did a job for a man in Texas once, Walt Coburn. Do you remember him?"

"Yes," Tracker said. He remembered Coburn, all right. His daughter had been killed during a bank holdup, and he had hired Tracker to bring back the man that did it. There were two of them, and Tracker had ended up killing them both. "Yes, I remember him."

"Well, he's a friend of mine, and he gave me your name. It took me a while to track you down, but then word gets around, and I finally heard you were here."

"I'm sorry if the trip was wasted," Tracker said, "but I don't hunt men anymore. Not like that."

"Well, maybe if you let me tell you what my problem is, my trip may not be wasted."

"It can't hurt to listen, I suppose," Tracker agreed.

"Good."

"You mentioned the Blue Cut job," Tracker said. "That rings a bell, but I still can't recall—"

"You might have read it in the newspaper," Duncan said. "It was in Missouri, in the area of Glendale. A train was stopped in a ravine called Blue Cut, and held up. It's reputed to be the last job pulled by the James gang."

"That's right," Tracker said, remembering now. He had read about it in a newspaper. "But that was in September of eighty-one, wasn't it?" he asked.

"Yes," Duncan said, "six months ago."

"Were you on that train?"

"I was, and I lost something that is of great value to me. I wanted to hire you to get it back for me."

"After six months?" Tracker asked. "Who knows where the James gang is now? They could have all split up."

"You needn't find the whole gang, just Jesse. He's the one who took it from me."

Fine, Tracker thought, just Jesse.

"What was this valuable item that Jesse James took from you, Mr. Duncan?"

"It was a gold—uh—pocket watch," Duncan said.

29

"What?" Tracker said, not sure he'd heard right. "You want to hire me to go after Jesse James because he took your watch?"

"That's right, Mr. Tracker," Duncan said. "My watch."

[6]

Tracker poured them both another drink while they discussed the matter further.

"Mr. Duncan, maybe I'd better explain to you what it is I do now," Tracker said. "You see, if you had lost something of great value I would go and get it back for you...for half. The chances of failure would be very slim, but if I should fail, you wouldn't have to pay me anything. But a watch..."

"All right, what about this?" Duncan asked. "I'll pay you ten thousand dollars to get me that watch back."

Ten thousand dollars was a lot of money for a watch. There had to be more to it than that.

"Ten thousand just for a watch?" Tracker asked. "There must be more to it than that."

"Twenty thousand, then. I must have that watch back. It has no monetary value that I can split with you, but I'll pay you twenty thousand." Duncan was getting anxious again, like Duke had said he was the day before.

"This watch means an awful lot to you," Tracker said.

"Yes it does. I asked Jesse James not to take it from me, but he seemed to delight in doing so. The more it meant to me, the more he wanted it."

"You should have told him it was broken," Tracker suggested.

"Yes, that's what he said, too."

"So let me get this straight. You're offering me twenty thousand dollars to get this watch of yours back from Jesse James."

"Right."

"You don't want me to catch Jesse or any of his gang?"

"No, not at all. All I want is the watch. I don't care if Jesse James and his gang are never caught."

"Do you want to tell me what it is that makes this watch worth twenty thousand dollars?"

Duncan hesitated, then said, "It's worth that much to me, Mr. Tracker, and I can afford to pay that much."

That was probably the only thing that did make sense to Tracker. If Duncan could afford to pay twenty thousand, then the watch was worth at least that much—to him.

"What if I find Jesse and he has the watch?" Tracker asked. "We might have to buy it back from him."

"Well, if that's—wait a minute," Duncan said.

Tracker didn't wait, though, because he knew what Duncan was probably thinking.

"I'm not trying to hike the price on you, Mr. Duncan," Tracker assured him. "Look, you'll just let me know where you're going to be and if I have to buy the watch from Jesse, I'll send you a telegram telling you how much he wants. If you think I'd use that arrangement to hike my own fee, then maybe you should hire someone else."

"No, no, of course if you have to buy it— Do you think he'd really sell it to you?"

"I'm just exploring a possibility."

"Does this mean you'll take the job?" Duncan asked.

It was then that Tracker realized that he had decided to take the job, for several reasons. One was the twenty thousand dollars, another reason was the prospect of meeting Jesse James, who had been called the most hunted outlaw ever.

His final reason, however, was the fact that he had been in San Francisco, and inactive, for too long. He needed something to get him back on the go again.

Why not get paid twenty thousand dollars while he was at it?

[7]

Tracker and Duncan agreed that half the money would be paid in advance and the other half upon completion of the job. However, if he failed, the first half would be returned.

"I'll be staying at the Alhambra. I have some other business in San Francisco that should keep me here until the end of next month. If you have to get in touch with me, contact me there."

"Meet me here tomorrow morning," Tracker said, "with cash. Remember that. No checks."

"I'll pick the cash up from my bank and have it for you by tomorrow. Thank you, Tracker."

"Thank me when I come back with your watch," Tracker said. The two men shook hands and then Duncan left.

Tracker sat down, shaking his head. A watch, he thought. I'm going to look for Jesse James and face him for a watch.

And for twenty thousand dollars.

He decided that this was too good not to share with Duke, so he went down to look for him.

He found him in the lobby.

"Duke," he said, getting his friend's attention. "Let's go into the saloon. I want to buy you a drink and tell you a story."

"Oh?" Duke said. "You mean you're going to share your business with me?"

"Believe me," Tracker said, laughing, "this is too good not to share."

Five minutes later, over two beers at a corner table, Duke said, "You're crazy, Tracker."

"No, but if I stay around here much longer I will be," Tracker replied.

"Yeah, but Jesse James?"

"I'm not after Jesse James, Duke, I'm only after that watch."

"And that's crazy, too. I mean, Jesse is supposed to have the watch, isn't he?"

"So? The man is a thief, isn't he? I'm sure if he knows he can turn a profit from that watch he'll jump at the chance."

"He's also a killer, Tracker. What about that?"

Tracker's eyes seemed to shine as he said, "Yeah, what about that?"

"Tracker, you don't know Jesse James, do you?" Duke asked suddenly.

"No, I don't know Jesse," Tracker said, drinking some of his beer, "but," he added, putting the mug down, "I do know Frank."

"What?" Duke asked, giving his friend a shocked look.

"I met Frank James once, a few years ago," Tracker explained. "If I find Jesse, and Frank is there, I'm sure we'll be able to work something out for the watch."

"Without anybody getting killed, hopefully," Duke said.

"I'd have to agree with that," Tracker said.

"So that's why you accepted the job," Duke said. "It might end up being a lot easier than it sounds."

"Well," Tracker admitted, "it would be easier if, when I found Jesse, Frank was with him."

"Sure," Duke said, no longer as worried. "Sure, it'd be a cinch."

Sure, Tracker thought, as Duke went for two more beers.

If Frank remembers me.

Part Two

[8]

Glendale, Missouri
March 25, 1882

It had been a long time since Tracker had ridden his horse, Two-Pair, such a long distance, and it felt good. He had taken the train from San Francisco as far as Kansas and ridden the rest of the way. He wanted to take a look at the ravine called Blue Cut before going on to Glendale. It didn't tell him much, but it gave him a starting point. Once he left Blue Cut for Glendale, it was as if his job had officially begun.

Before leaving San Francisco, he had read as much as he could about the Blue Cut job, but he knew that nothing he read would be able to tell him as much about it as the law in Glendale, Missouri, would. If they would. Tracker had had trouble with the law before, as far as getting information, but then that had been when he was a bounty hunter. Maybe now it would be different.

When he rode into Glendale, uppermost on his mind was a drink, so he dropped Two-Pair—who was named for the hand with which he had won him in a card game—at the livery stable and made for the nearest saloon.

"Beer," he told the bartender, "as cold as you can get it."

"It's good and cold, mister," the bartender assured him. When he put it down in front of him he found that

37

the bartender was right. One look told him it was cold, and then one taste told him that it was good.

"Now, that's what I like," Tracker said, "an honest bartender."

The bartender smiled, nodded, and went down the bar to tend to another customer. By the time he came back, Tracker had emptied the mug and he asked, "Can I get you another?"

"Maybe later. Right now I could do with some directions."

"Sure. Where you wanna go?"

"Well, you could tell me where a good hotel is, and then you could direct me to the sheriff's office."

"Want to give yourself up?" the bartender asked, laughing at his own joke.

"Not hardly."

"Well, they're both in the same direction. Go out the door here and make a left, walk about two blocks, and you'll come to the hotel. It's on this side of the street. The sheriff's office is about a block further, and it's across the street."

"Okay," Tracker said. "Much obliged...and I'll be back later for that second beer."

"See you then, mister."

Tracker took his saddlebags and left, heading for the hotel. He had no trouble finding it, and asked the clerk if he could get a room facing the street. There was no problem with that, and he went on up to his room, dropped his saddlebags to the floor, and stretched out on the bed. He didn't realize how tired he had been until he woke up about an hour later.

"Shit," he said out loud, "I must be getting old."

He stood up and walked to the window to look out at the main street.

He leaned his hand against the wall next to the window and ran his other hand over his face. After all that time spent in San Francisco, with all those people around him—Duke, Deirdre, Shana, Will, and the other members of the hotel staff—it was good to get out again, to be alone again.

He backed away from the window, picked up his hat, and left the room. Time to go and talk to the sheriff.

He walked out the front door of the hotel and crossed

the street diagonally, which left him right in front of the sheriff's office. He knocked on the door and entered.

"Sheriff?" he asked the man behind the desk.

The man was young, in his late twenties, and it was more likely that he was a deputy.

"Naw," the man said, "I'm jest the deputy," confirming Tracker's theory. "Kin I help ya?"

"No, I wanted to talk to the sheriff," Tracker replied. "Do you know where he is?"

The deputy seemed to make a concerted effort to think over the question, then said, "Well, it's startin' to get dark, so he's prob'ly making his early rounds. Why'n't you try the saloon? He'll show up there sooner or later."

"I'll do that. Thank you."

Inside, the deputy walked to the window and watched Tracker walk to the saloon. He searched through his memory, wondering if there was a wanted poster on the man. Man that big, he had to get into trouble some time or other. Ah hell, the deputy thought, walking back to the desk, even if he was wanted, the sheriff wouldn't do nothing, anyway.

Tracker walked into the saloon and ordered that second beer he said he'd return for.

"That's what I like," the bartender said, putting it down in front of him, "an honest customer."

"Thanks," Tracker said. "Has the sheriff been in yet?"

"You mean for his early drink during early rounds?" the barkeep asked. "No, not yet. Should be in any minute now, though."

"Thanks. I'll wait at a table."

"Sure thing."

Tracker took his beer to a corner table and sat facing the door, with his back flat up against the wall. Off to his right there was a small poker game going on—four men playing for small stakes—and after he talked to the sheriff, he thought about sitting in to while away the time. He didn't intend to stay in Glendale more than this one day and night, unless something happened to change his mind.

The level on his beer was halfway down when a man wearing a badge walked through the bat-wing doors and up to the bar. He was a large-boned man with gray

39

hair peeking out from beneath a weathered hat, and he had the florid, flushed face of a man who liked his liquor.

"Let me have my early one," he was saying to the bartender as Tracker walked up next to him, carrying his beer.

"Sheriff?" he asked.

The lawman virtually ignored Tracker until the bartender had set his rotgut in front of him and he had taken a healthy drink, draining the shot glass.

"Again, Ernie," he said, and then he finally turned to Tracker and said, "Jesus, you're a big one, ain't you? I'm Sheriff Finster. What can I do for you, stranger?"

"Well, I'd like a few minutes of your time to ask you some questions, Sheriff. My name's Tracker."

"Tracker, eh?" the sheriff said. The bartender put the second drink down in front of him and the sheriff wiped his mouth and then downed it.

"I'm doing my rounds now, ya know," the sheriff said.

"I'd only need a few minutes, Sheriff," Tracker said. "I'd be willing to spring for a drink or two."

That piqued the sheriff's interest. His face acquired a crafty look and he said, "Well, I might be able to spare you a minute or two. Pour me another, Ernie, on the stranger." As the bartender poured the drink the sheriff asked Tracker, "What would this be about?"

"It's about the Blue Cut robbery," Tracker said, and both the bartender and the sheriff froze just long enough for Tracker to notice.

"The Blue Cut robbery?" the sheriff asked. "Not the Glendale train?"

"The Blue Cut job, Sheriff," Tracker verified. "September sixth. Can we talk?"

The sheriff hesitated, and Tracker didn't know why, but he wanted to talk to the man, so he said to the bartender, "Why don't you give us a bottle of that stuff, Ernie," and threw some money on the bar. "You can refill my beer, too."

As the bartender handed Tracker a bottle, the big man noticed Sheriff Finster's eyes following the transfer from Ernie's hand to his own.

"Bring your glass, Sheriff," Tracker said and walked

back to his chosen table. The sheriff followed and sat opposite Tracker, with his back to the door.

"Have a drink," Tracker said, pouring one.

"Thanks."

"Sheriff, I'd like to know what, if anything, you've been able to find out about the gang who held up that train at Blue Cut."

"What's to find out?" the man asked. "It was the James gang, pure and simple. There ain't no secret about that."

"I know that, but have you heard anything about the gang since then?"

"Well, there was an arrest. Fella named Matt Chapman was arrested and he admitted that Frank and Jesse was there."

"Is that so?" Tracker asked, with interest. "Did you arrest him?"

"Me? No, it wasn't me," Finster replied. "He was arrested by Jim Timberlake, the sheriff over to Kansas City."

"I see."

"Yeah. As a matter of fact, the whole investigation— of both train robberies—was handled over to there. They got what you call a po-lice commission or some such thing."

"Police commissioner?" Tracker asked.

"That's it. I guess that's progress for ya, eh?"

"And the whole matter was handled from there?"

"Still is being handled from there, I reckon," Finster said. "They ain't caught Jesse yet, has they?"

No, Tracker thought, they haven't, and if everything is being handled in Kansas City, then I'm wasting my time here with you, you old lush.

Tracker stood up, annoyed at the drunken sheriff and at himself for wasting time and money.

"Hey, you ain't gonna take that bottle, are you?" the sheriff asked, touching his mouth with his fingers.

"I sure as hell am, Sheriff," Tracker said. "You've got rounds to perform, remember?"

The sheriff stared after Tracker as the big man

walked over to the poker table, said a few words, and then sat down and poured everyone a drink from *his* bottle.

There oughtta be a law, he thought bitterly.

[9]

Captain Henry Craig was annoyed. Irritation was his usual reaction every time he got a message that Jim Timberlake was coming to see him. True, Craig was the police commissioner and Timberlake was just the sheriff of Kansas City. Timberlake, however, was close to the governor, and for that reason he invariably acted as if he and not Craig were the superior.

Of course, the plan to kill Jesse and Frank James was Jim Timberlake's, and Craig admitted—albeit to himself—that it was a good one. The James brothers had been thorns in Missouri's side for long enough. In the past, governors like Hardin and Phelps had withdrawn all the rewards that had been issued on the James boys and their gang, but when T. T. Crittenden had entered the governor's office, he had issued a reward for fifty-five thousand dollars for the entire gang, and five thousand extra for Frank and Jesse.

Still, no one had been able to collect as yet, and then last year the gang had the audacity to pull two train robberies within two months of each other. That was the last straw, and the governor had been about to double the reward money when Jim Timberlake voiced his idea.

Kill them. That's right, just kill them, and use members of their own gang to set them up for it.

It was Timberlake who had discovered that the James

brothers were frequent visitors to the home of Bob and Charley Ford, and it was he who had gone to their sister, Martha Bolton, to tell her that her brothers ought to go and see the governor in connection with a plan to capture Frank and Jesse James, for which they would each receive ten thousand dollars in reward money. The meeting had been held, and the Ford brothers had agreed. Craig was sure that the Fords had other reasons to go along with the plan, but he didn't care what they were. As long as they did it, as long as they helped to kill Jesse James—with or without his brother, Frank—or even killed him themselves, that was all that mattered.

Once that was done, maybe Craig could finally put Jim Timberlake in his proper place.

Jim Timberlake was on his way to see Henry Craig, always a distasteful task for him. He didn't like the police commissioner, and he had plans, through his relationship with his "friend" the governor, to oust Craig and become police commissioner himself.

The reason he was going to see Craig now was the telegram in his hand, which had been sent from Glendale by that drunken lawman, Finster. It seemed there was a "big man" in town asking about the James gang and now he was on his way to Kansas City, although how he knew to come here, Finster swore he didn't know. Timberlake knew, though. That idiot had probably been so drunk he didn't know what he was saying, but whatever it was, it was leading this "big man" right to Kansas City, just when they didn't need anybody snooping around.

Planning to kill the James brothers was fine, but they didn't need anyone finding out that it was a scheme upon which the sheriff and police commissioner of Kansas City, and the governor of the state of Missouri, were not only agreed, but were also deeply involved.

Timberlake knew some of the other reasons why the Fords would be willing to go along with the plan. He didn't know the details, but one of the Fords had killed a man named Wood Hite, who was a cousin to Jesse and Frank. For that reason they were afraid that Jesse might come after them, so it made sense for them to get him first. Also, Jesse had been at their house looking for a man named Jim Cummins, who was apparently shooting his mouth off about some of their jobs. When Jesse asked another Ford, this one a fourteen-year-old named Albert, where Cummins had gone, he said he didn't know. Jesse, apparently not satisfied with that answer, had taken young Albert out in the woods and tried to torture the information out of him. This gave the Fords another reason for wanting Jesse dead, and that was revenge. The offer of the money was the push the Fords needed to go ahead and get it done—although God knew when they'd do it. Timberlake still wasn't sure that they would be able to overcome their fear of the famous outlaw and actually kill him. If it worked, however, he would be sitting pretty, because the whole scheme had been his idea.

Maybe then he'd finally be able to get rid of Henry Craig and become police commissioner himself.

Governor T. T. Crittenden was hopeful that Jim Timberlake's plan would work, and that Missouri would finally be rid of the Jameses. As he sat behind his desk in the governor's mansion in Jefferson City, tugging at his muttonchops, he realized that the plan was a daring one. If anyone should find out that he had sanctioned employing the Fords to kill Jesse James, his career would be finished—and he'd make damned sure that Craig and Timberlake went down with him.

If it worked, however, then people in the East would no longer look upon Missouri as a lawless state and businessmen would flock to invest their money in making Missouri a great state, and at the same time making T. T. Crittenden a great governor.

And maybe...a great President?

It all depended on Jesse James—a dead Jesse James!

Bob and Charley Ford sat in a small house on a hill behind the town of St. Joseph, Missouri, and each had his own thoughts about what they had agreed to do. They were both frightened—more frightened than they had ever been before in their young lives. Ten times a day they each thought, What if he knew? What if Jesse knew about what they were planning to do? And what

45

if he knew that they—one of them, anyway—had killed his favorite cousin, Wood Hite?

There was no doubt about what had to be done. This was one thing the brothers Ford agreed on.

They had to get Jesse before he got them.

And what was Jesse James, the infamous outlaw, thinking? He was living under another name in St. Joseph, Missouri, with his wife and son, and he wished that Frank were there. Frank, however, was fighting the consumption, and he had gone to Texas with his family to rest.

Rest.

That was a word Jesse James did not know the meaning of. Even Frank, his older brother, had found time to rest, but not Jesse. No, never Jesse. Jesse had to be the strong one, the decision maker.

Why? Why did Jesse always have to be strong, even when he was just plain dog tired?

Why? Because that was what Jesse James demanded of himself.

And what Jesse James demanded, Jesse James always got, right?

Right?

[10]

Tracker was surprised to find Kansas City such a large place. He had been there once before, years ago, when it was just a small town. But like many small Western towns it had grown, just as the West itself was growing. How long would it be before there would be no notice-able difference between the East and the West? Why should two halves of one country be so different?

Tracker took Two-Pair to the livery and then went in search of a hotel. There were enough to choose from, and in the end he decided that one was probably as good as another, so he chose the Kansas House hotel and requested a room fronting the main street.

He stopped in his room just long enough to drop off his saddlebags and rifle, and then he went in search of a saloon.

Again, as with the hotel, there were a fair number of saloons in town, so he chose the one with the loudest music and the brightest lights.

"A beer," he told the bartender. When he tasted it he found that it wasn't as cold or as good as the one he'd had in Glendale. They probably watered the liquor here too, he thought.

"Can you give me directions to the sheriff's office?" Tracker asked the bartender.

"Sheriff Timberlake's office?" the man said. "Why, sure."

Kansas City might have been five times as large as Glendale, but the directions to the sheriff's office were just as easy to follow. The saloon was on the main street and so was the sheriff's office. In fact, so was the police commissioner's office, which was in something called the Municipal Building.

Tracker finished his beer and thanked the bartender for the directions. He walked down the street a few blocks until he came to the sheriff's office, then knocked on the door and walked in.

The man behind the desk stood up and studied Tracker intently. He was a large man, not as tall as Tracker but taller than average, and he wore a worn Colt on his hip. He had bushy brown eyebrows and an even bushier mustache.

"Can I help you?" the man asked.

"Are you the sheriff?"

"Yes, I am. My name's Timberlake, Sheriff Jim Timberlake," he answered. Timberlake put his hand out, and Tracker came forward to shake it. "What might your name be?"

"My name is Tracker."

"Well, Mr. Tracker," the sheriff said, letting go of Tracker's hand, "you just arrive in town?"

"Yes."

"Well, I wish every stranger would come to my office as soon as they arrive in Kansas City," Timberlake said. "It would make keeping tabs on everything a whole lot easier."

"I didn't just come to check in with you, Sheriff," Tracker said. "I have some questions I'm hoping you might be able to answer."

"Is that so?" Timberlake replied. "Well, then, why don't you have a seat and tell me what's on your mind. Sorry I can't offer you a drink, but I don't keep any in the office."

"That's okay."

"Now then, what's on your mind?" the lawman asked.

"I'm looking for some information about a train robbery that was supposedly pulled by the James gang."

"The James gang," the sheriff repeated. "Well, we've had our fair share of train robberies here in Missouri."

"I'm more concerned with the Blue Cut job," Tracker told him. "That was the most recent one, wasn't it?"

"Recent, yeah," Timberlake said, scratching his cheek, "but still some time ago." The sheriff peered carefully at Tracker, then asked, "You aren't a bounty hunter by any chance, are you?"

Tracker shifted uncomfortably in his chair and said, "No, I'm not." He hoped that the question was just one of idle curiosity, and that the sheriff had not somehow recognized his name.

"Then what is your interest in the James gang and the Blue Cut robbery?"

"Well, to be absolutely frank with you, Sheriff, I've been hired by someone who was on the train to retrieve something that was stolen from him."

"After all this time?" Timberlake asked. "I'm sure any money the gang might have gotten from that job has long since been spent."

"Well, this item was not cash—"

"Still, what makes you think any of the gang would still have—uh—whatever this 'item' is, after all this time?"

"Well, I'm not getting paid to think they still have it, I'm getting paid to find out for sure, and if so, get it back."

"Uh—the man who's paying you, does he have any idea which of the gang might have taken it?"

"He said the leader."

"Jesse?"

"If it was the James gang, then I guess that would mean Jesse, yes."

"Oh, it was the James gang, all right. Nobody but Jesse would be fool enough to hold up a train only two months after another robbery, and in the same region. That's Jesse for you."

"I guess he must be a pretty brave man," Tracker said. He said it because he wanted to observe Timberlake's reaction to the remark.

"Brave?" the sheriff said. "I don't think that's the word I would use to describe a thief and a murderer, Tracker." The sheriff seemed annoyed, but he quickly recovered his composure. "Foolhardy," he went on in a

49

calmer tone, "that's what I would call Jesse James. Just plain foolhardy."

"I understand he's become quite a legend here in Missouri," Tracker said. "That there are actually people who help him escape, or avoid, capture."

"They are foolhardy as well, Mr. Tracker. They're taken in by the romantic notion that the James boys are merely misunderstood victims. Once they're brought to justice, the people will sing a different tune."

"Well, I wish you luck," Tracker said. "I have no desire to bring anyone to justice. I simply wish to retrieve what was lost by my client."

"I see. Well, how do you intend to do that?" the sheriff asked. "Just ask Jesse for it? And how do you intend to find Jesse?"

"I was hoping you would give me some help."

"Me? How?"

"I'd like to see your records on the investigation following the Blue Cut robbery. It might give me some idea as to where Jesse went afterwards."

Timberlake stroked his mustache as he mulled over Tracker's request.

"I don't see any harm myself in letting you see my files," he finally said.

"Good."

"But I would have to clear it with Captain Craig."

"Captain Craig?"

"He's our police commissioner. I'm sure that's an unfamiliar term to you, but back East every city has a police commissioner to oversee their law-enforcement agencies. Our governor thought it would be a good idea if Kansas City, as well as some of the other larger towns in Missouri, had a police commissioner."

"I see."

"In any case, I'd have to clear it with him first. Suppose I get back to you tomorrow. How would that be?"

"That'd be just fine," Tracker said, rising. "And in the event he refuses, do you think I'd be able to talk to him myself?"

"Well," Timberlake said, also standing, "why don't we cross that bridge when we come to it? Where are you staying?"

"At the Kansas House."

"Fine hotel," the sheriff said, walking Tracker to the door. "Wonderful food. Why don't you enjoy all the pleasures that Kansas City has to offer tonight, and I'll get back to you tomorrow, after I talk to Captain Craig."

"I appreciate it."

"I'll do what I can," Timberlake promised.

Standing outside the sheriff's office, Tracker had the impression that Sheriff Timberlake was much too smooth an operator. He also had a feeling that the man was not surprised by his appearance or his request.

He wondered if that drunken fool Finster had wired ahead that he was coming to Kansas City.

He wondered if he was really going to get any cooperation at all, and if not, why not?

Why not, indeed?

[11]

"The man is dangerous," Timberlake told Captain Henry Craig only an hour after Tracker had left his office.

"How do you know?" Craig asked.

"You've only got to look at him to know," Timberlake said.

"Then maybe he'll find Jesse and kill him for us," Craig proposed. "He'd be helping us and not even know it."

"Our plan has already been put into effect," Timberlake argued. "We don't need anybody snooping around and messing things up."

"Then what do you propose?"

"I think we should not give him any information that might lead him to Jesse," the sheriff said, "but I've sent a telegram to the governor to see what he wants to do."

"I don't think we should be contacting the governor every time we have to make a decision," Craig said. "We don't want him to think—"

"The governor likes to be kept aware of everything that is happening," Timberlake reminded Craig, "especially when it concerns Jesse James."

"Still, I think—"

"Do me a favor, Craig," Timberlake said, heading for the door, "Don't think. I'll let you know when I get word from the governor."

With that, Timberlake left Craig's office and slammed the door behind him.

Craig marveled at the fact that every time he saw Timberlake, the man managed to make him hate him a little bit more. He knew the man wanted his job, but he wasn't going to let it go that easily. First they'd finish this fight against Jesse James, and then they would fight each other. He knew he was at a disadvantage, since Timberlake was the governor's man, but he wasn't about to give up without a fight.

Outside the Municipal Building, Tracker watched as Timberlake came out and walked back to his office. Something was up, that was for sure. He had followed the sheriff first to the telegraph office and then to the Municipal Building, where he had no doubt that he was the topic of conversation between the lawman and the police commissioner. A short conversation at that, for Timberlake came out after about fifteen minutes.

Tracker watched as a light went out on the top floor of the building. He figured that was where the commissioner either had his room or his office. He filed the information away for future reference.

What confused him slightly was the sheriff's trip to the telegraph office. Who was he sending a telegram to, and what about? Was he sending information to someone, or was he asking for instructions from someone?

He moved out of the darkened doorway he was standing in and decided that this time he really would go over to the saloon and enjoy the pleasures that Kansas City had to offer.

Whatever Timberlake was up to, Tracker decided he would still wait and see what the man had to say in the morning.

Timberlake had one more stop to make before he called it a night.

"You just want me to take the guy to bed?" Amanda Locke asked.

"That's it, Mandy," Timberlake said.

Mandy Locke lived in one of the sleazier hotels in Kansas City, on what some people called "the wrong side of town." She was a short, buxom blonde who made her living on her back, and did an occasional "favor" for Sheriff Timberlake because she knew better than to refuse.

"That's all. You don't want me to—"

"I just want to know where he is, that's all," Timberlake told her. "And if you are your usual charming self, I'm sure I'll know where he is, at least until morning."

She smiled with her unbelievably talented mouth—which talents Timberlake had sampled many times in the past—and said, "In bed."

"In bed," Timberlake repeated.

Governor Crittenden read the telegram from Jim Timberlake again and then put it down on his desk. He was wearing a dressing gown, and had been interrupted from his dalliance with a woman very much like Mandy Locke by the messenger who brought the telegram. First he read it in his apartment, but once he knew what it said, he told the young lady he'd be right back and went to his office to read it again.

The name "Tracker" meant nothing to him, but by morning it would, because he was going to have his assistant check him out thoroughly.

Before he made any kind of decision on how to deal with Tracker, he wanted to know who he was dealing with.

[12]

The woman probably thought Tracker was a fool, but so what? Let her. Tracker was sure that Mandy Locke had been sent to him by Sheriff Timberlake, either to get some information out of him or to make sure he stayed in one place. Tracker was only too happy to go along with it.

"In we go, Mandy," he said, as he opened the door to his hotel. There was a slutty sexuality about Mandy that whetted his appetite, and appetite that had not been satisfied since he had left San Francisco.

"Nice room," she commented.

"It's okay."

"I don't get to this part of town all that often," she told him.

Looking at her, admiring the large, firm globes of her breasts, which were very much in evidence, what with the low-cut dress she was wearing, Tracker decided that he should enjoy the night, and that maybe she should as well.

"Come on, Mandy," Tracker said reproachfully. "I'm sure Timberlake has sent you here before, to entertain other guests."

"Timberlake?" she asked. "You mean the sheriff?"

"Of course I mean the sheriff," he said. "Your friend and mine."

"I don't understand. I just saw you in the saloon and thought that we could have a good time together—"

"Mandy, you and I could have a nice time here tonight. All we have to do is understand each other."

"I'm afraid I still don't—"

"You were sent to me by Timberlake," he said, and explained his reasoning. "My guess is he doesn't want me wandering around, so you're supposed to keep me in one place."

She frowned at him and said, "And you don't mind?"

He walked up to her and plucked her shawl from her shoulders. Now they were as naked as the slopes of her breasts. He ran his finger down between the cleavage of her breasts and said, "Why would I mind? I've known worse ways to spend a night."

"Come down here, Mr. Big Man," she said, reaching for his neck. He bent over and their mouths melded together. Her hands became busy, undoing his buttons. He returned the favor. In no time at all they were both naked, and he picked her up. For someone so full-bodied, she was surprisingly light in his arms, and he carried her to the bed.

When they were on the bed together her hands traveled down between them and she began to caress him, saying, "My God, you're big all over, aren't you?"

She bent over him and proceeded to show him what a talented mouth she really had. She worked his shaft in and out of her mouth until he became impatient and reached for her. He practically lifted her up, then, and impaled her on his rigid penis.

"God!" she cried out as he worked her up and down his shaft, at times thrusting so deeply inside her that she thought he would split her in two.

"Mister...God...you're doing it to me...God..." she moaned. It had been a long time since San Francisco for Tracker, and he wasn't able to hold back as long as he would have liked. He shot his load into her like a geyser and she threw her head back and almost bit through her bottom lip in an effort not to scream.

"Jesus, mister," she said a few moments later. She was still sitting astride him, and she said, "It's still hard," wiggling her hips.

Tracker reached up and cupped each of her plump

breasts in his hands and said, "We've got all night, Mandy." He massaged her breasts and she started to moan and move her hips again.

"Oh, mister..." she groaned.

"In the morning you can tell Timberlake you really did your job tonight," he told her, tweaking her large nipples.

"Ooh, and enjoyed every minute of it," she said, leaning over so he could take her breasts into his mouth.

[13]

The next morning Sheriff Timberlake was watching the Kansas House hotel from across the street when Mandy Locke walked out. She spotted him across the street and gave him a nod, which gave him no indication at all of what kind of a night she'd had. Jesus, she had to go home and get some rest.

Satisfied that Tracker was still inside, Timberlake walked over to the telegraph office.

"Stan, any telegrams for me?" he asked the operator.

"Yeah, Sheriff. Matter of fact, I just finished taking it down," the man said, handing a slip of paper to Timberlake. The sheriff read it twice, then folded it up and put it in his shirt pocket. His next stop was Captain Craig's office. He and the police commissioner had more problems than they thought.

Tracker woke up that morning only long enough to watch Mandy get dressed and leave. She asked if they would get to see each other again before he left town, and he said he'd have to let her know what his plans were. She told him where she lived and then left. He turned over and went back to sleep for an hour, then got up, ravenously hungry. A night like the one he had just spent with Mandy Locke would do that to a man.

He decided to take Sheriff Timberlake at his word and had breakfast right there in the Kansas House dining room. He was glad to see that the sheriff had at least been honest about the food in the hotel. The steak was tender and the eggs were firm, the way he liked them. Also, the coffee was good and strong.

He wondered if the sheriff and the commissioner had decided yet whether or not to let him look at the files on the Blue Cut job.

It would certainly make things a lot easier, no matter what their reason was.

"Have a cup of coffee," Craig told Timberlake.

Timberlake knew that Craig was trying to out calm him, and he couldn't let the man do that. He knew it was childish, but two men who were in competition with each other often acted like two boys competing.

"Black, thanks," Timberlake said.

"Have you heard from the governor?" Craig asked.

Timberlake had an advantage here. He already knew what was in the telegram. He decided to let Craig read it for himself and watch the man's face while he did.

"Here's his answer," he said, handing the esteemed police commissioner the telegram.

The sheriff sipped his coffee and watched the police commissioner's face while he read what the telegram said about Tracker. It said that the man had a reputation for being a hard case, and for getting his job done. It said that no one seemed to know which side of the law he was on, if indeed he had ever picked a side. He used to be a bounty hunter, but had dropped out of that business only recently. The governor ended his telegram by saying he did *not* want Tracker to interfere with their plans in any way!

Craig put the telegram down and looked at Timberlake. Only then did he become aware that the other man had been watching his face the entire time. He tried to keep a placid look on his face, but his voice shook when he spoke.

"This man is dangerous, Timberlake," he said.

"I know that, Craig," the sheriff said. "I've met him, don't forget."

"Then what are we going to do about him? If he's around when our plan goes into effect—"

"Our plan has already been put into effect, Craig,"

59

Timberlake said. Scratching his chin, Timberlake continued, "I'll have to tell him that the files he's interested in have been sent to Jefferson City, to the governor's mansion."

"And what if he goes there?"

"Well, if he goes there, he's the governor's problem isn't he?"

"Crittenden won't—"

"If he's in Jefferson City, Craig, he'll be that much further away from Jesse James, won't he?"

"I suppose so," Craig admitted.

"Yeah, you suppose so," Timberlake muttered, standing up. "The longer we keep Tracker away from Jesse, the better chance we have of having the life of Jesse James end before this man can ruin our plans." He gave Craig a disgusted look and said, "I'll keep you apprised of what happens, Craig. Thanks for the coffee."

With that Timberlake turned on his heel and left Craig's office. Craig took out a pen and a piece of paper and began composing a telegram of his own. He wanted to make sure that if the roof fell in on this whole thing, he wouldn't be under it.

[14]

After breakfast Tracker thought that Timberlake should have had sufficient time to know whether or not he was going to give Tracker a look at those files. Tracker paid his bill and left the hotel.

Kansas City was already showing some signs of life. The larger cities of the West come to life much earlier than the smaller cities and towns do, because they are striving to make themselves even larger and more prosperous. A dead town looks dead, no matter what time of day it is. The same can't be said for a prosperous, growing city.

Tracker stepped into the street, waited for a loaded buckboard to go by, and then crossed. He walked to the sheriff's office and entered without knocking.

The sheriff's office and the Municipal Building had in common the fact that they were both brick structures, something one didn't see much of in the West— the old West. Tracker had seen them aplenty in San Francisco, and he knew there were more in the East, but these structures had only just begun to make their way west.

Timberlake was seated behind his desk, reading some papers, and he looked up as Tracker entered.

"Well, good morning, Mr. Tracker," he greeted him.

"Just Tracker will be fine, Sheriff," the big man said.

61

"Did you have a good evening last night?" Timberlake asked.

"I did, thanks to you."

"I'm sorry," the sheriff said, looking perplexed, "I don't understand."

"That girl you sent me, she was a very good choice. She really knows her stuff."

"Girl?"

"Mandy Locke, Sheriff. Let's not play games, please."

"Did she tell you—"

"She didn't tell me anything, Sheriff, so don't take it out on her," Tracker said. "I'm simply not a fool."

Tracker watched Timberlake's mind work, and saw the man change rails quickly to accommodate the situation.

"Well, I never thought you were, Tracker," he said. "I simply felt it my duty to see to it that you had a nice evening. I'm glad I succeeded."

"Sure. Thanks. Now what about getting a look at those files? Did you discuss it with Police Commissioner—what's his name?"

"Craig, Captain Henry Craig," Timberlake supplied. "Yes, as a matter of fact, I spoke to him early this morning."

As well as last night, Tracker added to himself.

"And?" he asked.

"Well, I'm afraid this isn't going to be exactly what you want to hear, Tracker."

"Just give it to me straight, Sheriff, don't try to spare my feelings."

"Well, it seems that the police commissioner, Captain Craig, has sent those particular files—uh—the ones you're interested in—to the governor's mansion in Jefferson City by special messenger."

"Is that a fact?"

"Yes, it is. It seems the governor requested that he do that, and even though Governor Crittenden called it a request..." And Timberlake spread his hands in a helpless gesture as he let the sentence trail off. "I hope you understand," the sheriff added, as if as an afterthought.

"I'm afraid I don't," Tracker said. "It seems odd to

me that the police commissioner wouldn't have told you about that as soon as he did it."

"I can't speak for Captain Craig, and I can't reprimand him, since he's my superior."

"When were these files sent to Jefferson City?" Tracker asked.

"Oh," Timberlake said, making a show of thinking the question over, "some time last week, I believe he said."

"I see."

"I'm really sorry about this, Tracker. I understand your disappointment, naturally."

"Naturally."

"I hope you'll understand."

"I'll try to console myself," Tracker replied, thinking this was a foolish game for two grown men to be playing.

He stood up and said, "I guess I better think about taking a ride to Jefferson City to see the governor. Do you think he'll let me see the files?"

"I try never to predict what our governor will or won't do, Tracker. The man has a mind of his own."

Tracker started for the door and Timberlake stood up to accompany him.

"When will you be leaving?" the sheriff asked.

"In a hurry to see me go?"

"Hah, not at all. I thought maybe if you liked our city you might stay a few extra days. I'm sure Mandy wouldn't mind visiting you again."

"That's not a bad idea," Tracker said, looking as if he were giving it some serious thought. "Maybe I'll stay today and leave tomorrow morning, first thing."

"Sure. Enjoy what our city has to offer for one more day," Timberlake said, clapping Tracker on the back.

"I'll do that, Sheriff," Tracker said. "I'll enjoy *everything* this little town of yours has to offer."

[15]

"A favor?" Mandy Locke asked Tracker. "What kind of a favor?"

It was after dark now, and Tracker and Mandy Locke were seated together in the same saloon where they had "met" the night before.

"Tell me something, Mandy," Tracker said. "What do you really think of Sheriff Timberlake—just between you and me, now."

"Just between you and me?" she asked, wary of saying anything against Timberlake that might get back to him.

"It won't go further than this table," Tracker promised.

She thought it over for a few more moments and then said, "I think he's a pig. That's what I really think of him."

Now that she had said it, she looked around hastily, to see if anyone might have overheard.

"It's all right," he assured her. "Nobody heard you. Relax."

"That's hard to do in this town," she said. "Not with Timberlake and Craig."

"Are they close friends?"

"Friends? Hah! They hate each other."

"How do you know that?"

"I've spent some time with the sheriff when he's had

a few drinks," she said. "When he's drunk, he talks, and what he talks about is how much he hates Craig, and how he intends to get his job."

"I see," Tracker said, filing that information away for further reference.

"All right, Mandy. This is what I want to do," he said, and went on to explain his plan to her. She listened intently, and Tracker had the feeling that she might not be as dumb as she acted. Her lack of intelligence might have just been part of her whore guise.

"Timberlake would kill you," she said when he finished talking.

"You let me worry about Timberlake," he told her.

"He'd kill me."

"He won't touch you," he said. "I promise."

He gave her time to think about it and ordered a couple of more drinks while she did.

"You know," she said finally, "this might be worth the risk, just to see Timberlake's face."

"If he ever finds out about it," Tracker said. "And don't you ever get reckless enough to tell him about it."

"Not unless I'm holding a very big gun," she said with feeling.

"Then it's a deal?"

"For two hundred dollars?"

"Right."

"And when you come back, we can—" she started to ask.

"Yes," he assured her, "we can, and will."

"When do we go?" she asked, suddenly eager.

"In a little while. Let's drink up and make it look good. He'll be watching us when we leave, I'm sure, and I want him to feel very sure that we're going to be in for the night."

After that, Tracker became very loud, and even joined a poker game, with Mandy at his elbow. He made sure that everyone knew what he and Mandy meant to do when they left there. And finally, when it was close to midnight, he staggered out of the saloon with his arm around Mandy's shoulder, one hand firmly clasped around one plump breast. He wanted his meaning to be as clear as a bell, and when he and Mandy Locke walked through the front door of the Kansas House hotel, he could feel Sheriff Timberlake's eyes on his back. He hoped Timberlake was satisfied that Tracker was going to be very busy for the remainder of the night.

[16]

Tracker indeed intended to be very busy for the rest of the night, but what he had to do could not be done inside his hotel room. He needed Mandy Locke's cooperation, though, to be able to succeed with what he had to do. He didn't need her to swear he was in the room with her all night, should the necessity arise. What he needed was for her not to say that he *wasn't* there all night. She didn't have to say anything unless Timberlake hit her with a direct question, and then it was up to her what her answer would be. However, two hundred dollars and a chance to do something against Timberlake had assured him of her cooperation, at least on this night.

Half an hour after they had entered his room, Tracker climbed out a back window of the hotel and dropped to the ground below. He did not even want to take a chance on being seen using the back door.

Once on the ground, he carefully worked his way to an alley, and then to the front of the hotel. After assuring himself that the street was empty, he hurried across to the other side and hid himself in a darkened doorway there. Satisfied that he had gone undetected, he worked his way around to the rear of the sheriff's office.

Even though the building was made of brick, the door was no better than any other door. It posed no problem for a man of Tracker's size and strength to force it open.

Knowing that at least one deputy had to be inside the office, Tracker paused to see if he had been heard. When he was sure he was still safe, he closed the door behind him and looked around the room he found himself in. As he had hoped, he was in a file room. Off to his left was a door leading to a block of cells. He checked the door between the front room and the back by putting his ear against it. He thought he could hear someone snoring on the other side. Everything was working tonight, and that was fine with him. He might as well enjoy it, he thought, since he knew from experience that sometime in the future things would even out and something would go against him.

He examined the room and found a shirt hanging on the back of a chair. He used it to block the crack at the bottom of the door so he could light a lamp without it being seen beneath the connecting door. Once that was done, he found a kerosene lamp and lit it, keeping the flame low but still bathing the room in enough light to see. That done, he began going through a file drawer, looking for a file on the Blue Cut robbery, or on the James gang. He hoped that Timberlake had merely lied to him about the file, and had not thought to actually remove it. His hope was realized when he found a file on the James gang, which included a report on the Blue Cut robbery.

Tracker again put his ear to the connecting door to satisfy himself that the deputy on the other side was still snoring, and then settled down to read the file.

It took him the better part of an hour to read all of the file, but when he was done he was sure he had all the information he would need. He had reassembled the papers and was replacing the file when the connecting door between that room and the front room began to creak open. He turned to see the door opening slowly, as if the person on the other side was not sure what he would find. There was no time to douse the light. As the barrel of a gun became visible, Tracker knew what he had to do. He couldn't risk being recognized.

He covered the distance between himself and the

door in two giant strides and grabbed the wrist of the hand holding the gun. The other man grunted as he felt the strength of Tracker's grip. Tracker pulled the man into the room, making sure that the gun never pointed at him. The man lost his balance and stumbled into the room. Tracker followed quickly and threw a hard right to the back of the man's head. The blow caused the deputy to lose his grip on his gun, and Tracker quickly kicked it across the room. As the deputy struggled to his feet, Tracker stepped back, poised for a clear blow at the man's face. Just as the man was about to look up at his face, he hit him with a vicious left that knocked him back and out. Tracker checked to make sure he was unconscious but alive, and then blew out the lamp and quickly left.

He worked his way carefully back to the rear of his hotel and climbed up to the second-floor window he had exited from, hoping that no one had closed the window behind him. Finding the window open, he entered, walked back down the hall to his room, and let himself in.

Mandy Locke was still there, still naked and still in his bed. She had been dozing and came awake as he entered.

"Did you get what you wanted?" she asked.

"I sure did," he said, starting to undress. After his recent exertions, the sight of her plump, pink-tipped breast and the light thatch of hair between her rounded thighs excited him.

"Then come here," she said, putting her arms out, "and give me what I want."

He moved into the circle of her arms and began to kiss the firm flesh of her breasts while one hand dove between her thighs, finding her wet and ready. While he licked and sucked at her nipples, causing her to moan and clutch his head tightly in her hands, he began to manipulate her with his fingers. Soon her crotch was moving against the pressure of his hand and she was moaning and begging for him to do it to her. Tracker was exhilarated by his short fight with the deputy and the return to a lush, naked woman in his bed. He wanted this to last.

He continued to kiss her breasts and then moved his

lips down over her belly. He could smell the sharp scent of her, and he was going to do something he only did when he was very excited.

He moved down even further, until he was able to taste her and plunge his tongue into the warm depths of her.

"Oh, God," she moaned, "what are you doing..."

He knew just what he was doing, and he knew what it was doing to her. This was something he had done on occasion with Shana, but never with Deirdre. He didn't know how Deirdre would react should he even suggest it.

It was good, though, and it was definitely something he was going to have to try with her, sooner or later.

Mandy Locke's pleas fell on deaf ears, and it was not until he was ready that Tracker removed his mouth and replaced it with his penis. He drove himself into her almost brutally, and she raised her hips to meet his thrusts. He reached beneath her to cup her fleshy buttocks and knead them roughly as he continued to drive into her.

"Oh Lord, Tracker," she said. It was if she were calling him her Lord for what he was doing to her. This was the most incredible sex she'd ever had with a man, and she wanted it never to end. Finally, she could feel him swell tremendously inside of her, and then release himself into her. She tried to milk as much of that burning-hot fluid out of him as possible, and then she felt as if her whole body were going to burst...

"My God," she said afterward, "where did you learn to do that? It was—I've never felt anything—" She stopped herself short and turned her head to look at him as they lay side by side.

"I guess you think I say that to everyone that I— It must be funny, coming from a— Oh, I'm not really a whore, you know. Please, say you know.... Even if you have to lie."

If she knew it was a lie, he didn't see how his saying it could satisfy her, but as part of her payment for helping him, he tried to make it sound as sincere as possible. He said, "Yes, I know."

[17]

The following morning, as badly as Tracker wanted to get started right away, he forced himself to take the time to have breakfast.

He went to the hotel dining room and ordered his usual, and as he expected, Timberlake came walking in before he was finished. Spotting Tracker seated in the corner, the lawman walked purposefully over to his table with his hand on his gun.

"Good morning," he said.

"Good morning, Sheriff," Tracker replied. "Take a seat. Have a cup of coffee, on me."

Timberlake did not reply to the invitation, but pulled out a chair and sat down.

"Still leaving this morning?" he asked.

"Uh-huh," Tracker replied around a mouthful of steak and eggs.

"Going to Jefferson City?"

Tracker swallowed first, washed it down with a sip of coffee, and then said, "Yep."

"Did you have a nice night?"

"Very nice," Tracker said. "Incredible, in fact. That Mandy is a very talented girl."

"Yes, she is," Timberlake said, but he had something other than Mandy's talents on his mind, and it showed plainly on his face.

"All night?"

"Every minute of it," Tracker said, trying to look very pleased with himself. "You never know when the next time will be."

"I suppose," Timberlake commented. He's wondering how to bring it up, Tracker thought, and continued eating.

Scratching his nose, Timberlake finally said, "You know, we had a very odd occurrence last night."

"Is that a fact?"

"Yes. Someone broke into my office."

"Your office?" Tracker said, sounding surprised. "That takes a lot of nerve, breaking into the sheriff's office."

"Yes, but that's not the oddest part of it."

"Oh, no?"

"No," the lawman said, shaking his head. "The oddest part is that whoever it was roughed up my deputy, and then didn't steal anything."

"Well, that makes sense."

"It does?"

"Sure. Your deputy must have scared him away."

"I don't think that's likely," Timberlake said. "Whoever he was, he knocked my deputy out, and did it easy as pie."

"Maybe you need a new deputy," Tracker suggested.

"Maybe I do."

Timberlake decided to accept Tracker's offer of a cup of coffee and poured himself one. He took a sip and then set the cup down on the table.

"You wouldn't know anything about that, would you, Tracker?" he asked.

"What, about the break-in at your office?" Tracker asked. He shook his head slowly and said, "No, I don't think I know anything. I didn't see anything, if that's what you mean, but then, I'd had a little bit to drink, and I had something else on my mind, you know?" Tracker gave Timberlake a man-to-man smile that the sheriff did not return.

"Sheriff, you're not suggesting that maybe I broke into your office, are you?" Tracker decided to ask.

Timberlake tried to look surprised and didn't succeed.

"I hadn't really thought of it, but now that you mention it..."

72

"Was there anything in your office that would be of any interest to me?"

"No," Timberlake said, shaking his head. "Not a thing."

"Well, then, that answers that," Tracker said. He put down his fork and wiped his mouth with a napkin. "I guess it's time to go. Is there anything else, Sheriff?"

"Yes," Timberlake replied, "there is." He waited a long moment and then said, "Give my regards to the governor."

"I'll do that, Sheriff," Tracker said, rising. "I surely will."

Timberlake watched Tracker walk out of the dining room and said, "Sure you will, you bastard."

[18]

"Why didn't you arrest him?" Police Commissioner Craig demanded.

"For what?" Timberlake asked, looking at Craig with undisguised distaste. "For outsmarting us?"

"For assaulting a deputy."

"My deputy never saw who hit him," Timberlake said in a tired voice. "The best he could do was to say that it might have been a big man."

"You let him ride out of town, Timberlake, and you know damn well he's not going to go to Jefferson City. Why the hell didn't you take that file out of your office and hide it, or burn it?"

"Because *we* didn't think of it, friend," Timberlake said. "Remember, I'm not in this alone, you know. It's you and me, working for the governor."

"Sure, while he sits in his mansion with his hands clean," Craig said bitterly. As soon as he said it he wished he could take it back. There was no point in giving Timberlake more ammunition with which to get his job from him. He saw Timberlake's mind snap at the remark and file it away for future use against him.

Damn the man! Why did he let him get him so angry that he didn't know what he was saying?

"What are we going to do now?" Craig asked.

"I think we're just going to have to wait," Timberlake

said, "and hope that those Ford boys can get the job done before Tracker can manage to mess it up."

"Damn it, Timberlake, you know where Tracker is headed now," Craig moaned.

Yep, I know where he's headed, Timberlake thought. He's headed for Saint Joe, Missouri, and if we're lucky he'll ride right into the middle of a hornet's nest . . . and get stung to death.

Part Three

[19]

St. Joseph, Missouri
March 28, 1882

Apparently, the governor's push for progress had even reached St. Joseph, Missouri. Tracker had expected to find a one saloon, one hotel, one horse town, but instead found a thriving city. It was not Kansas City, but it *was* a city, and not just a town.

Tracker quickly ran the gamut of livery stables, hotels and saloons, finding one of each for his use and settling down in the latter with a cold beer.

As hard as it was for a man of his size to keep a low profile, that was what he was going to try to do. He had very little conversation with the bartender and simply picked out a corner table from which he could observe and listen.

The first thing he planned to do was just wait and see if he spotted Frank James. If Frank was in town, he would have to show up at the saloon sooner or later.

The notes he had found in Timberlake's file had helped him to pinpoint St. Joe as the town where the James boys might possibly be hiding out. As a result of the investigations of the Glendale and Blue Cut train robberies, Timberlake and other law enforcement officials, including railroad detectives and a Pinkerton agent hired by the railroad, had all agreed that Jesse and Frank James had very probably not left Missouri.

The final decision by all these "great brains" was that Jesse and Frank would probably hide out in the small town of St. Joseph. What surprised Tracker was that the file suggested that Jesse and his family might even have lived in Kansas City for a time, immediately following the Blue Cut robbery.

The file ended showing that, by direct request of Governor Crittenden, the railroad and Pinkerton detectives had been withdrawn from the investigation, leaving it in the hands of Police Commissioner Captain Henry Craig and Sheriff James Timberlake, both of Kansas City.

Finishing his beer, Tracker wondered why, if Timberlake and Craig thought that Jesse was in St. Joseph, they hadn't taken some kind of action by now. He himself had only been in town the better part of an hour, but he knew that something wasn't right. He could feel it. Tension and fear were both very heavy in the air.

He had gone to the bar for a second beer and reclaimed his table when two young men walked in and walked to the bar. They seemed to be known to the bartender, who greeted them both, though not with any degree of warmth. One appeared to be about twenty-one, and the other a few years older. It was obvious that they were brothers, the resemblance was that strong.

What struck Tracker most about these two men, however, was their edginess—or perhaps "wary" was a better word. At the slightest sound they would both jerk their heads around, to see the cause. Tracker, at one point, deliberately scraped his chair back, and they turned and eyed him anxiously, and then curiously. He held their gaze for a few moments, until they both turned away and concentrated on their drinks.

Very nervous young men, indeed.

After that, they finished their drinks in a hurry and then quickly left the saloon.

Bob and Charley Ford had not liked the looks of the big man who had been sitting at a corner table in the saloon.

"What if Jesse sent him?" Charley Ford asked.

"Why?"

"Because he knows, Bob. He knows what we're planning, but he doesn't want to kill us himself."

"Jesse does his own killing," Bob Ford reminded his brother. "Don't worry, Charley. We'll get Jesse before he gets us."

"Yeah," Charley replied. "Sure."

They walked along in silence for a few moments, and then Bob Ford revealed his own concern over the big man's presence in the saloon.

"Still," he said, "I wonder who that fella is, and what he's doing in town."

"It doesn't have to have anything to do with us or Jesse," Charley Ford replied.

"I guess not," Bob said, "but I'd still like to know who he is. Let's check with the hotel," he suggested to his brother. "Won't do no harm to find out his name."

"No harm at all," Charley agreed.

[20]

Tracker sat in that saloon long enough to eventually be accepted as a fixture. The bartender stopped shooting glances over his way, and a little later on he was even invited to fill in a chair at a poker game. He accepted.

He paid attention to the talk that went on at the table between the other three players, but never once were Jesse or Frank James mentioned, and he himself did not want to introduce their names into the conversation. Not just yet, anyway.

He played halfheartedly, losing more often than he won, keeping an eye on the door, examining every man who came in for a drink, but never once did he see anyone remotely resembling Frank James. He wondered how much Frank would have changed over the years, but felt sure that he would still be able to recognize him.

Tracker had not told Duke when or how he had come to meet Frank James, but now he thought about it. It was in April of 1874, when Tracker had still been a bounty hunter. He had been tracking a gang of killers across Missouri, and had caught up to them around Kearny. "Caught up" was not exactly the right way to put it. He had been pinned down by them in a ravine just outside of Kearny and he had been running low on shells. He knew that as soon as they figured out he was out of shells they'd rush him and kill him. But before that could happen a rider came up behind the four gang members and suddenly it was they who were under fire, caught in a crossfire. The gang quickly mounted up, and as they rode away the lone rider picked one of them right off his horse. The others kept riding and were quickly out of range.

The rider had then ridden up to Tracker and said, "You want to go after them?"

Tracker looked at the man and the way he was dressed and said, "You look more like you're dressed for a wedding, or something."

"I am," the man replied. "My brother is getting married, in Kearny. That's just a few miles from here."

"Well, I'm much obliged for the help," Tracker told him. "I'll take up after them as soon as I buy me some extra shells."

"Here you go," the man had said, tossing Tracker a box of shells. They were .45's, just what Tracker's pistol and rifle used.

"Will you let me pay you for these?" Tracker asked.

"Nope. I'm in too good a mood," the man said. "You sure you couldn't use some help tracking those fellas down?"

"No. I'm usually much better at my job than this situation would indicate," Tracker told him, loading his rifle and handgun. "I appreciate the offer though. Why don't you go on to your brother's wedding, and give the bride an extra kiss for me."

Smiling broadly, the man said, "I'll do that. What would your name be, by the way?"

"Tracker," he answered, stepping up to the man to shake his hand.

"You a bounty hunter?"

"Yep."

"Guess I'm lucky that you're busy, then," the man said.

"Why is that?" Tracker asked.

"My name's Frank James."

Frank James watched Tracker with an expectant look on his face, for Tracker was still holding his handgun. Holstering it, Tracker said, "I don't collect prices on the heads of men who save my bacon, friend. That

83

brother of yours who's getting married, that would be Jesse, then?"

"That's right."

"A little risky, ain't it?"

"Not in Missouri," Frank answered. "We got too many friends here."

"You and your brother thinking of settling down?"

"Maybe," he said. "Maybe we'll talk about that at the wedding. Speaking of which, I better get going before I'm late. I'm the best man."

"Again, I'm much obliged for the help, and the shells."

"My pleasure. You watch your step, Tracker, and if you need any help while you're in Missouri, just tell folks you're a friend of Frank James."

"Thanks."

With that, Frank James, one of the West's most notorious outlaws and killers, rode off to Kearny, Missouri, where his brother Jesse was getting married.

There was a lot of money waiting in Kearny for an ambitious bounty hunter that day, but Tracker threw the dead man up on his horse, mounted his own, and rode the other way.

Sitting in a saloon in St. Joseph, Missouri, now, he remembered what Frank James had told him that day about needing any help while he was in Missouri.

He wondered if anyone at that poker table, or in that saloon, or in the whole town of St. Joseph, would believe him if he told them that he was a friend of Frank James.

[21]

March 29, 1882

In the café at breakfast the next morning, he noticed that there were people talking with their heads together, looking at him. Someone who had seen him in the saloon the day before had mentioned him to someone else, and the word was getting around town now, in spite of his attempt to keep a low profile.

That's what you get, he thought, when you're six foot four and slightly worn out.

He decided to get a haircut and a shave after breakfast, and then went over to the saloon and took the same table.

By early afternoon a man wearing a badge walked into the saloon and looked around. When he saw Tracker, he walked to the bar, got himself a drink, and then carried it to Tracker's table.

"Have a seat, Sheriff," Tracker said before the man could speak, "I've been expecting you."

The sheriff, a tired-looking man in his mid-forties, tall and thin with a heavily lined face, replied, while seating himself, "Don't mind if I do."

"Word been getting around?" Tracker asked.

"Yes, sir, that's why I'm here. I wanted to take a look myself, and have a little chat with you."

"About what?"

"About what you're doing in St. Joe."

"Right now I'm having a beer."

"And that's all you did yesterday, too."

"That's not exactly true," Tracker said. "Yesterday I played some poker, too."

"And paid more attention to the door than you did to your cards," the sheriff added.

"Somebody's very observant, Sheriff," Tracker remarked. It was then that he wondered if the sheriff had gotten a telegram message from Kansas City.

"What's your name, by the way?" Tracker asked.

"Green, Jed Green, Mr. Tracker," the man replied.

"Just Tracker, Sheriff."

"Got your name from the hotel register."

"I see." Either that, or from Timberlake's message.

"Would you mind telling me why you're here in St. Joe, Tracker?" the sheriff asked.

"You mean you don't know?" Tracker asked. "Didn't Timberlake tell you in his telegram?"

"Timberlake?" Green snapped, looking as if he wanted to spit all of a sudden. "If I ever got a telegram from Timberlake I'd burn it before I'd read it."

"Not on good terms, huh?"

"Not with that jackal. You have a run-in with him in Kansas City?"

"We talked."

"He send you here?"

Tracker shook his head.

"I had enough of the big city. I wanted something smaller and more comfortable."

"So you ain't gonna tell me why you came to St. Joe?"

"Sure, Sheriff," Tracker said, "I'll tell you. I came to buy a watch."

The sheriff stared at Tracker and then finished his drink. Standing up, he said, "All right, keep your reasons to yourself. As long as you don't cause no trouble, you're welcome to stay, but at the first sign of trouble—"

"I know," Tracker said, "out I go."

"I may not look like much, mister," Sheriff Green said, "but I know how to do my job."

"I'm sure you do, Sheriff," Tracker replied. "You can count on me. No trouble."

"I'll hold you to that," Green said, and left.

People just naturally never seemed to believe you when you were telling the truth.

[22]

By the end of the second day, Tracker was relatively certain that Frank James was not in St. Joe, Missouri—but that didn't necessarily mean that Jesse wasn't. Without Frank there, though, he was going to have to alter his tactics. He wondered idly if Frank had ever mentioned the man he'd stopped to help on the way to Jesse's wedding. If Jesse remembered the incident, it would again make things easier, but he couldn't count on that.

One way he might be able to find Jesse was to approach every man in town and ask him the time, then examine his watch. That would be tedious—and maybe a little silly—but he didn't discount the possibility altogether.

That night, in his hotel room, Tracker sipped rotgut from a bottle while he gazed out the window at the darkened street below. He had a feeling that Jesse James was in this town somewhere. It was not something he could explain, but if Jesse was there, that might explain the tension and fear he felt in the air.

He had not seen the two nervous young men from the first day in the saloon, and he wondered about them. He wondered if they would have been edgy enough to have asked about him after they left the saloon.

He put the bottle down, strapped on his gun, and went down to the front desk.

The clerk was an elderly man, and Tracker knew that he would probably respond to either force or money. He decided to use money.

"Hello, Pop," Tracker greeted him.

The old man looked up at him and said, "Evenin', youngster," with the emphasis on *youngster*.

Tracker smiled and said, "I didn't mean to insult you, friend."

"You didn't," the old man told him. "You only called me what everybody else calls me. What kin I do for you?"

"Not for me," Tracker told him. Showing him a dollar, he said, "I want to know how many people have been here asking about me since I arrived, and I'll give you a dollar for each name."

Tracker saw the greed light up the man's eyes and knew that he was about to receive the names of everyone who lived in the town.

"Of course, if you lie to me, I'll eventually find out, and I'll come back and make you eat every cent you cheated me out of."

Tracker's eyes bored into the old man's moist, rheumy eyes until he looked away and said, "I ain't gonna cheat ya, sonny. Ask away."

"I already did," Tracker said. "Who's been asking about me since I arrived in town?"

"Well, the sheriff was here, asking what I knew about you," the old man said.

"What did you tell him?"

"I showed him the register," he answered, touching the book. "That's all I know about you."

Tracker dropped a dollar into his hand and the old man's fingers closed around it like a bear trap.

"Okay, who else?" Tracker said, taking out another dollar piece.

"You might need two more of those," the man told him.

"Why?"

"Well, the Ford boys, they came in together, even though it was only Charley who talked. That would count as two, wouldn't it?" the desk clerk asked eagerly.

"The Ford boys?" Tracker asked. "Two young men with mustaches, dark hair, and a bad case of nerves?"

"That's them."

"Sure, Pop," Tracker said, giving him two dollars. "That's worth two. Thanks."

Tracker started back to the stairs, when the old man called him back.

"I ain't done yet," he complained.

"What?" Tracker asked. "There was someone else?"

"Yep," the old man said, putting out his hand. Tracker took out another dollar and held it up in front of the man's face.

"Who was it?"

"A lady," the old man said, widening his eyes, "a blond lady, very pretty. Wanted to know who you was and how long you was staying."

"What was her name?"

"Well, I don't know her, but I've heard other people call her Zee. Her last name's Howard."

"Zee Howard?" Tracker said. The man nodded, and Tracker handed him his dollar.

"Thanks, Pop," he said. "You earned your money."

He went back to his room and resumed his former position at the window with the bottle.

He'd found out what he wanted to know, that the Fords were nervous enough about something to check up on the stranger in town. There was a new development, though, and that was the blond lady. Who could she be, and why would she be interested in him? Was she friend or foe?

The sheriff had asked about him because that was his job.

The Fords because they were nervous about something.

What was her reason?

Zee Howard.

The name meant nothing to him.

[23]

March 30, 1882

The next morning Tracker decided to go looking for Zee Howard and find out why she had been asking about him. Where to start looking, though? That was the question.

He had breakfast in the café and decided against asking about her there. He'd been in town too long to claim that she was a friend or a relative. The people in the café had seen him for three mornings now, and would wonder why he hadn't asked before. He was going to have to find someone who hadn't seen him yet, who he could ask without arousing any suspicion.

As he left the café his eyes fell on the dress shop across the street, and he knew that was the place. The only problem was that there was no way he could go in there without looking out of place. Since there was no way to avoid that, he crossed over and went on in.

He took off his hat and began to browse around, while the ladies in the store looked him over. The elderly woman behind the counter kept an eye on him while she finished taking care of two women. When she was finished, the women exited giggling, and she approached Tracker. "May I help you?" she asked, her tone dubious.

"Um, yes, ma'am. I'm looking for a—uh—a gift."

"A gift?"

"Yes. Something small but pretty. It's for my cousin. She lives in town."

"I see. Could you tell me something about her? What color hair does she have? How tall is she?"

"Uh—she has blond hair," Tracker said. He had no idea how tall the woman was, so he brought her name up earlier than he had intended. "Maybe you know her? Her name is Zee Howard."

"Oh, of course, I know Mrs. Howard," the woman said, warming immediately. "She's your cousin?"

"Yes, and I've just arrived in town and I'd like to get her a present before I see her."

"Well, I think that's a lovely idea," the woman said.

"Nothing very—uh—large, you understand. Maybe just a ribbon for her hair? Just something to tell her that I'm glad to see her after all these years."

"Oh? How many years has it been?" the woman asked.

"Uh—oh, a lot—a lot of years. Since we were ...younger," Tracker stammered.

"Well, pink is a wonderful color for Mrs. Howard," the woman said. She picked up a pink length of ribbon and held it out for him to see. "How about this one?"

"That's perfect," Tracker said. "Now that this problem is solved, I only have one other."

"Oh?" she asked, walking behind her counter. "What is that?"

"Where cousin Zee lives," he said. "I had a letter from her, but I lost it and now I can't remember her address." Tracker tried to sound very puzzled and unhappy.

"Oh, well, that's no problem at all," the woman said. "I can tell you where she lives."

"You can? That would be very nice of you," Tracker said.

"Not at all. What would Mrs. Howard say if I let her cousin wander around town looking for her? She lives on Lafayette Street with her husband, Thomas. I believe the number is thirteen-eighteen."

"Thirteen-eighteen Lafayette Street," Tracker repeated. "I can't thank you enough."

"Not at all," she assured him. He paid her for the ribbon and left, thanking her again for "cousin Zee's" address.

Outside, he shoved the ribbon into his pocket and then started off in search of Lafayette Street.

Number 1318 turned out to be a small wood-framed house that looked as if it had been poorly cared for. Tracker took up a position across from the house, having decided to take a wait-and-see attitude. The woman in the store had said that Zee Howard lived there with her husband. That had changed Tracker's mind about going right up and asking for Zee Howard and asking her why she was so interested in him. With her husband around, that wouldn't do. The woman would obviously deny ever having seen or heard of Tracker.

Better to stand and wait. If Mr. Howard was home, Tracker would wait for a more opportune moment.

His waiting finally paid off when he saw a man cross in front of a window, closely followed by a blond woman. He could tell nothing about them except that the man was bearded, the woman blond. Since it was early, he decided he'd wait a while more and see if the man would go out, giving him a chance to talk to the woman without her husband around.

Along about late afternoon the front door opened and a man came out. He was bearded, but Tracker assumed that this was Mr. Howard. He backed into the alley he was standing in and watched Howard start walking toward town. Tracker gave him a few minutes, then left the alley and walked across to the house.

He knocked on the door and waited, hoping the door wouldn't be answered by a man. It wasn't.

The woman who answered the door was blond and very pretty. She looked to be in her late twenties and had a very sturdy, attractive body. Her hair was almost the color of corn, and her eyes were blue and very pretty despite the fragile network of lines at the corners.

"Can I help you?" she asked.

"You can if you're Zee Howard," Tracker said.

"I am," she said, eyeing him carefully, "but I don't know you. How could I help you?"

"You could tell me why you were asking about me at my hotel," he told her. "I'm Tracker."

Her hand flew to her mouth, and then she tried to close the door on him, but he put his foot in the way.

"Please..." she said, pushing on the door.

"I want to talk to you, Mrs. Howard," he said.

"Please..." she said again. "I can't. Please..."

He couldn't understand why she was so...panicky. The woman was not at all familiar to him. He was sure he had never met her before, but he asked, "Have we met before?"

"No, no, we've never met. I don't know you," she said, trying to close the door again.

"Then why were you asking about me at the hotel?" Tracker asked.

She stopped pushing on the door and planted herself solidly, facing him.

"Mr. Tracker, I can't discuss this with you here," she said. "My husband might come back, and he's a very jealous man."

"So? What do you suggest?"

"Tomorrow."

"Where?"

"Go for a ride in the morning. About a mile south of town there's a small pond. Wait for me there."

"What time?"

"Early," she said, exasperated now. "I'll come early. After breakfast."

"I have breakfast at eight," he said.

"All right."

"If you don't come," he said, "I'll be back here tomorrow afternoon, husband or no husband."

"I understand. I'll come."

"All right," he agreed, not sure he was doing the right thing. It was possible that he should have pressed her right then and there for an explanation, but he decided to let it go for a day.

"Until tomorrow, then," he said.

"Please move your foot?" she asked. He did and she closed the door.

Tracker started walking back to town, and as he turned the corner of Lafayette Street he saw the bearded Mr. Howard approaching. They exchanged glances and Tracker tried to see underneath the bushy beard, but as best he could make out, he had never seen the man before. The other man nodded and Tracker returned the nod, and then they both continued going their own ways.

94

[24]

March 31, 1882

Tracker passed the remainder of the evening in the saloon, playing low-stakes poker with the same three men. He participated a little more in the conversation this time, but still could not manage to find an opening to bring up the James brothers—or the Ford brothers. He ended up winning about twenty dollars and then going to his hotel and to bed.

In bed he found himself thinking about Deirdre, and Shana, and the hotel in San Francisco. He tried to force his thoughts to other things, because thinking about them would mean that he might be missing one or all of them.

He turned his thoughts instead to Zee Howard and what she could possibly tell him tomorrow that would satisfy him. From that point, he decided to go to sleep, so he could wake up in the morning and find out.

In the morning, after breakfast, he went to the livery to get Two-Pair and then started to ride south. He had gone a half a mile when he pulled Two-Pair to a halt.

What if he were riding into some kind of an ambush? No, that wasn't— Mrs. Howard had set this up on the spur of the moment. She didn't have time to plan an ambush.

Unless she planned it afterward—but why would she? He had pretty much established in his mind that he had never before met either of the Howards, so why would they want to set him up to be killed?

Besides that, Zee Howard did not look like the kind of woman who would idly send a man to be killed.

Satisfied—just about—that he was not riding to his death, he started Two-Pair off at a trot again. He knew he'd probably be the first one to arrive, since Mrs. Howard was not all that anxious to talk to him, but she probably would come, just to keep him away from her house again.

He recalled a portion of a dream he'd had the night before, concerning Deirdre, and he wondered if maybe he had dreamt of her because he had come in contact with first Mandy Locke and then Zee Howard, both of whom were blond. Sure, that must be the reason he'd dreamt of her.

When Tracker came to the pond he dismounted and secured Two-Pair's reins. He then settled down to wait for the arrival of Zee Howard. He hadn't long to wait, because presently she came riding up on a big bay mare and dismounted.

She was wearing riding clothes, instead of the dress she had been wearing the day before. Today her figure showed much more.

As she approached him warily, he noticed that she was not wearing any kind of artificial coloring on her face, yet she looked flushed and very attractive.

"Mrs. Howard," he greeted her.

"Mr. Tracker."

There was a long silence between them until Tracker finally said, "Are you planning on talking to me today?"

"Oh, yes—" she said. "I'm sorry. You wanted to know—"

"Why you were asking about me at my hotel. I think we've established the fact that we've never met before."

"No, we haven't."

"And I don't recall ever having met your husband before," he added.

"You saw him?"

"Yesterday, after I left your house. He was coming back as I was leaving."

"Did he see you—"

96

"—leave your house? No. Would you like to answer my question now?"

"I—uh—Jesse James is my cousin," she stammered, watching Tracker for a reaction.

"Yeah. So?" he said, watching her as well.

"I said Jesse James," she repeated.

"I know who Jesse James is, Mrs. Howard, but would his being your cousin cause you to ask about me at my hotel?"

"Because—" she said, and then stopped short. She walked to the edge of the pond, then turned around and continued. "Because Jesse is such a—a wanted man that I'm just—just suspicious of any strangers who come to town."

"I see," Tracker said. "That's your explanation?"

"That's it."

"Is Jesse in town?"

She looked shocked at the question and said, "No, of course not."

"Then why are you so interested in strangers?"

Tracker saw that her mind was working very quickly, looking for an answer, and then she said, "Well, maybe I'm not really interested in all strangers."

"Is that so?" Tracker asked. "Are you trying to say that maybe you saw me on the street and became interested?"

She tried to look coy as she answered, "Maybe," but her heart obviously wasn't in it.

"Well," he said, taking a couple of steps toward her, "if that's the case." He reached her and slipped his arms around her waist, but she put her hands on his arms and pushed them away stepping back at the same time, saying, "Please."

"Not that interested, huh?"

"Look, I have to go," she said, walking toward her horse.

"Zee, I'm not satisfied with your explanation," Tracker said.

She mounted up and then looked back at him.

"Mr. Tracker, I'm sorry, but I have nothing else to say to you. And if you choose to come near me again, I'll have to tell my husband about it."

"That would cause trouble," Tracker said.

"For you," she answered, and wheeled her horse around and set off at a fast gallop.

It would have been no problem to catch up to her, especially on a horse as fast as Two-Pair, but he decided not to. It was obvious that to find out why she had been asking about him, he would have to deal with her husband. He might as well stay away from her and make sure that when he did deal with Mr. Howard, he wouldn't be dealing with a jealous or irate husband.

He mounted up and headed toward town himself, but at a much slower pace than hers.

He was going to have to pick a time and place when to approach Thomas Howard, but while he was waiting, maybe it was time to have a little talk with the Ford boys.

[25]

When Tracker got back to the livery stable, it was empty. The livery man was nowhere to be found, so he walked Two-Pair in himself and started to unsaddle him. He noticed that the bay mare that Zee Howard had been riding was back in a stall.

He put both hands on his saddle, and as he lifted it off the horse's back, he felt a cold circle of steel touch him behind the right ear, and he heard the sound of a hammer being cocked.

He was completely amazed that he had not heard a sign prior to that.

"Just hold onto that saddle, friend," a man's voice said.

"Don't hold too tight onto that trigger, friend," Tracker returned.

"Don't worry about me, worry about yourself, Mr. Tracker," the man said.

"What is it you want?"

"I want to know why you're bothering my wife," the man said.

Thomas Howard?

"Howard?" Tracker asked.

"That's right. You went to see my wife yesterday, and you forced her to ride out of town today to see you again. I want to know what it's all about."

99

"Uh—that's very easy to explain, Mr. Howard, but it would be even easier without that gun at my head."

"I think I'll keep my gun right where it is, Tracker, and see if you can satisfy me with an explanation. I hear you're a real dangerous man." That last remark was said with heavy sarcasm.

"Where did you hear that?" Tracker asked.

"Around."

"This saddle is getting mighty heavy," Tracker remarked.

"You're a big, strong man, Tracker. I'm sure you can hold it up a little longer...especially since your life depends on it."

The man sounded like he meant it.

"Okay, so you want to know about your wife and me."

Howard pressed his gun harder against Tracker's head and said, "I don't think I like the way you put that."

"Look, ease off, okay? I'll tell you what you want to know, but not like this." Tracker had made a decision, and he hoped he was making the right one. "I'm putting this saddle down. You want to pull the trigger, you go right ahead."

Tracker took two steps and put the saddle down. When he did, he felt the gun move away from behind his ear.

"I'm going to turn around," Tracker said.

"Go ahead."

Tracker turned and faced Thomas Howard, who was still holding his gun, a .45 Colt, aimed at him.

"Start talking," the man said. He was standing in the shadows, and all Tracker could really see was his mouth, surrounded by the beard.

"Look, your wife is Jesse James's cousin."

"So?"

"So, I'm trying to find him."

"You a bounty hunter?"

"No—I used to be, but I'm not anymore."

"Then why do you want Jesse?"

"I'd—uh—rather tell him that."

"Tell me."

Tracker studied the man and wished he could see

more of his face, especially his eyes. His eyes would tell him whether or not Howard would shoot or not.

"I don't know that you have the right to know what it is I want to tell Jesse," Tracker said.

"As you said, Jesse and my wife are cousins. I'm acting for her. She has a right."

"Okay, let's make a deal," Tracker proposed.

"What kind of a deal?"

"I'll tell you why I want to talk to Jesse, if you'll make sure that your wife passes the message on to him."

Howard thought it over carefully, and Tracker continued to try and see past the shadows to his face.

"I think I can virtually guarantee that Jesse will get the message," he finally said.

"All right," Tracker said. "One more thing."

"What?"

"Put up the gun."

There was a moment when neither man moved, and then Tracker watched as Howard's hand uncocked his gun and then replaced it in his holster.

"Okay," Howard said. "Let's have it."

"It has to do with the Blue Cut robbery," Tracker said. "Do you know about that?"

Howard seemed to find that question amusing and said, "Yeah, I know about that."

"Well, there was a man on that train who lost something very valuable to him. He hired me to get it back."

"And that's why you're looking for Jesse?"

"Yes. The man is convinced that Jesse is the one who took the item from him."

"Even if that's true, what makes him think that Jesse would still have it after all this time?"

Tracker shrugged.

"That's what he's hired me to find out," he explained. "If Jesse still has it, and if he'll part with it...for a price."

"A price?" Howard asked.

"Yes."

"How much?"

"That's between Jesse and me."

"Well, then, what's the item?"

Tracker shook his head and said, "That's between me and Jesse, too."

"What makes you think Jesse would part with this...item, whatever it is?"

"I don't *think* he will," Tracker said. "I'm just going to ask him if he wants to sell it. I'm not anticipating what his answer will be, either. I don't know him well enough. Do you?"

"Do I what?"

"Know him well enough to anticipate his answer?"

"I don't know what the item is, and I don't know how much money you're talking about, so how could I predict anything?" Howard asked.

"Exactly," Tracker said. "So why don't you have your wife pass my message on, and we'll see what the man says."

"What makes you think that Jesse won't just set up a meeting with you and then kill you?" Howard asked.

"Because I don't think that Jesse James—and his brother, Frank—are the indiscriminate killers they're made out to be."

Tracker still couldn't see the man's eyes, but he had the distinct impression that he was frowning.

"That's a different attitude," Howard said.

"You mean, for someone not from Missouri?" Tracker asked.

"I'll talk to Zee," Howard said. "It'll be up to her whether or not she'll want to pass this on to Jesse—if, in fact, she does have an opportunity to see him."

"You'll let me know?"

"I'll be in touch," he said. "Meanwhile, do me a favor, will you?"

"Sure."

"Stay away from my wife."

With that Howard turned and stalked out of the stable, and Tracker breathed a little easier.

He finished taking care of Two-Pair, and then left the livery himself. He wondered how serious Howard had been while he was holding that gun to his head.

He also thought that, even before trying to find out what the story behind the Ford brothers was, maybe he should look a little more closely into just who Thomas Howard was.

After all, for all he knew, Howard could have been Jesse James himself.

[26]

Tracker did not make a move toward finding out about Thomas Howard until that evening. Once again he joined into a low-stakes card game with his three "friends," but this time he controlled the conversation.

The three men he played with were all from town. Jake Loomis was a clerk in the general store, one of many jobs the forty-year-old man had held over the past few years. His drinking invariably got him fired sooner or later.

The second man was Wally Timms, and he owned and operated the gun shop. He was a man of about fifty who didn't carry a gun, even though he could take apart and put back together any make or model.

The third man, in his late twenties, was the youngest of the group, and he was the one who fancied himself a card player. Dave Williams had never actually said what it was he did in town, and neither of the other two men had mentioned it, either.

"I tell you," Tracker said after they'd been playing for about a half an hour, "I've been in town for about three days and I haven't seen any of your local girls who was better looking than my horse."

"Oho," Timms said. "You obviously ain't been looking in the right places, friend."

"Like where?" Tracker asked.

"Like Sadie's," Dave said. "They got some ladies there—"

"Ladies?" Jake Loomis asked, laughing. "You call what they got there 'ladies'?"

"Ah, you're just mad because they won't let you in there anymore," Dave told him.

"Hey," Loomis said, leaning forward, "I don't wanna go in there anymore."

"Sure," Wally Timms said, and he and Dave exchanged amused glances. Loomis looked as if he were going to get very angry, so Tracker interrupted before things could get out of hand.

"Well, I saw a real good-looking lady today, and it wasn't anywhere near Sadie's."

"Oh yeah?" Dave said. "Do you know who it was?"

"Yeah, I found out her name," Tracker said. "Zee Howard."

"Tom Howard's wife?" Wally Timms asked.

"I guess so," Tracker said. "She's got hair like corn, and her body's—"

"I wouldn't go talking about another man's wife like that if I was you," Wally Timms interrupted.

"Especially not Howard's," Loomis said.

"Quiet, you two," Dave Williams said, and both Loomis and Timms shut up.

"Wait a minute," Tracker said, trying to look and sound puzzled. "What's the problem here? A man should be flattered if other men admire his wife. What's with this Howard, anyway?"

"Nobody knows all that much about him," Dave said.

"Well, what's he do for a living?"

"Nobody knows that, either," Jake Loomis said, but he didn't go further when he got a hard look from Dave Williams. Tracker wondered why both Loomis and Timms seemed to respond like that to Williams's remarks and looks.

"As for knowing what people do for a living," Tracker said, "I don't know what you do, Dave. I know what Jake here does, and I know what Wally does, but not you."

"I could say the same for you," Dave replied. "What do you do for a living, Tracker?"

"What is this," Tracker asked, "a trade?"

"I guess you could say that."

"Who goes first?"

Dave sat back in his chair, reached into his shirt pocket, and took something out. It was a piece of metal, and he pinned it to his shirt. Then he looked at Tracker and said, "I guess you do."

Actually, Williams had already gone first. By pinning his badge on, he'd shown Tracker that he was a deputy sheriff.

[27]

"A deputy?" Tracker asked, putting down his cards. "Why has that been such a secret up to now?"

"Who said it was a secret?" Williams asked, putting his cards down as well.

"Well, you sure haven't been wearing that badge the last two nights we've been playing," Tracker said. He was trying to sound more indignant than he was. The truth of the matter was he didn't like the idea of having been fooled, even though he recognized it as his own fault. He had paid all three of these men very little attention, simply using them to help him blend into the background.

"I haven't been wearing it because it doesn't look right to be wearing it while I'm playing cards," Williams explained. "You still haven't answered my question. You put the sheriff off, but don't think I'm as easygoing as he is."

Tracker took a long hard look at Dave Williams. He saw a man in his late twenties who appeared to be very easygoing, but now that he knew he was a deputy, he saw him in a different light. Williams was tall and well built, and would probably be a formidable opponent in a fight. He wondered how well he handled that Colt that he wore strapped to his thigh.

From the man's remark about the sheriff, Tracker also guessed that he probably had ambitions of becoming sheriff himself. So that made him young and ambitious, and he probably *would* be harder to put off than the sheriff had been.

Tracker decided to give Williams a little more than he'd given the sheriff, and hoped it would satisfy him.

"You going to answer my question," Williams asked, "so we can get on with our game?"

"What I do for a living?" Tracker repeated.

"That was the question."

Loomis and Timms were watching both men very carefully now, waiting to see if a confrontation would develop. If it looked like guns were going to be drawn, they wanted to make sure they got a good head start at getting out of the way of flying lead.

"Okay, Dave," Tracker said. "For the sake of the game I'll answer your question. I retrieve lost or stolen goods."

"What kind of goods?"

Tracker shrugged and said, "Any kind. If you've lost something, or have had something stolen, you can hire me to try and get it back for you."

"And that's what you're doing in St. Joe?" he asked.

"The question was, what do I do for a living," Tracker reminded him. "I've answered it. Now let's play cards."

Williams looked as if he was going to protest, but then he stopped himself.

"All right, Tracker," he said, "we'll play cards, but we'll continue this conversation another time."

"We'll see."

"Count on it," Williams said, picking up his cards and looking at them again.

Tracker looked at his own hand, which was three kings, and went ahead and made the largest bet he'd made during the three days they had been playing.

"I bet a dollar."

[28]

That night, when Tracker returned to his room, Zee Howard came to see him.

He answered a knock on his door—gun in hand—and there she was, standing in the hall. She had done something to her face and hair and stood with her hands clasped behind her, her breasts thrust forward.

"Are you going to shoot me?" she asked.

He looked away from her at the gun in his hand, and then said, "No, of course not. Come in."

"Thank you."

As she entered, he checked out the hall, found it empty, and closed the door behind them. He walked to the bedpost to holster his gun, then turned to find her watching him with interest.

"What brings you here tonight?" he asked. "I didn't expect to get an answer so soon."

"An answer to what?" she said.

"Didn't your husband tell you that we had talked today?" he asked.

She looked puzzled and said, "No, I haven't talked to . . . Tom today." He thought that the hesitation before she said his name sounded kind of awkward, but attached no great importance to it at the time. "What did you talk about?"

"I think I'd better let him explain that to you, Mrs. Howard," he said.

"Call me Zee, please," she replied. "What's your first name, Tracker?"

"Just call me Tracker," he said.

She approached him and touched his arm, as if curious to see how it felt. She ran her hand up and down the length of it and said, "A man has to have a first name."

"Just Tracker," he said again.

She was a damned puzzling woman. Up until now each time he had seen her she had given the impression of being a shy woman, but now she seemed to be very forward, and he thought he knew what she had in mind.

She squeezed his right bicep and said, "You're very strong, and very big. Are you very big all over, Tracker?"

"Mrs. Howard—Zee—I don't quite understand this. Out at the pond, when I touched you—"

"I was thrilled," she said.

"You didn't act thrilled."

She shrugged and moved her hand up to his neck.

"Anyone could have been watching us there, Tracker," she said. "But no one is watching us here."

She put both of her hands behind his neck and pulled his face down to hers. Her mouth fastened itself to his and he put his arms around her, pulling her tightly to him. He felt her full breasts crush against his chest.

She removed one hand from around his neck and put it between them and her hand tightened on his hard penis.

"Tracker..." she murmured against his mouth. When she kissed him it was not just with her lips, it was with her tongue and her teeth. She chewed on him and sucked on him and kneaded him until he couldn't take it anymore.

"Zee," he said, pushing her away, "you're going to go too far for us to stop."

"I don't want to stop," she said dreamily. Her hands went behind her to unfasten her dress and she shucked her clothes quickly.

Her body was not perfect by any means. Her breasts sagged just a bit from their own weight, and her belly had a tiny roll around it. Her thighs were heavy, too. She could have stood to lose a few pounds, but right then and there she was the most erotic sight he had seen in some time. He thought that perhaps that was because she had been so unapproachable up until that moment. Her sudden wanton behavior was so out of character that it excited him even more than it normally would have.

Her nipples were pink and they blossomed as he watched. She walked back up to him again, leaving a small space between them so that she could work on his pants and belt. He started to help her, but she said, "Let me," so he stopped.

Slowly, she undressed him, just barely touching his flesh each time she removed an article of clothing. When she finally had him totally naked, she fondled his genitals with such a light, feathery touch that he thought he would explode.

They moved for the bed and fell onto it locked together, with Zee on top. She pressed her firm breasts into his face and he opened his mouth to receive their offering. He nibbled and sucked on both of her nipples, and fondled her until she just about lost control, rolled over on her back, and begged to be ridden.

He drove the length of himself into her as deeply as he could and her reaction was incredible. She began to buck wildly beneath him and he fought to stay on her. Her hands came around and began to rake his back painfully with her nails as he continued to pound away at her. Finally, when he came, he felt her spasm around him, and gradually her bucking stopped, leaving them both breathless and covered with perspiration.

It was possibly the most violent coupling he'd ever experienced.

[29]

April 1, 1882

Tracker's sleep that night was alarmingly deep, and when he woke he was alone and could not remember when Zee Howard had left him. They had coupled once more that he could remember, and it had been as hellish a ride as the first time, leaving him drained and tired.

He struggled from the bed and stood up. His back felt stiff and sore and he was sure he had more than a few scratches and welts there.

There was something wrong in what had happened the night before, but he was in no shape to think about it now. At least not until he'd had some food and a lot of coffee.

He dressed, strapped on his gun, and started for the café. His shirt brushed painfully against the scratches on his back, and he wondered if he should go and find a doctor to have them treated.

Hunger won out and he continued on to the café, where he ordered his steak-and-eggs breakfast and a pot of strong coffee. Halfway through his second cup he felt as if he just might be able to think straight, and began to ponder about last night.

Zee Howard had been an almost entirely different woman than she was the first two times they spoke. Now, maybe it *was* because they were in his room where no one else could see them, but somehow he doubted it.

There was something behind her actions, and he wanted to find out what it was.

When he came out of the café he noticed Deputy Dave Williams standing across the street, leaning against a post, looking very relaxed. Tracker crossed over and confronted the young deputy.

"Are you keeping an eye on me, Deputy?"

"Yep," Williams said, smiling. "I told you we were going to finish our talk, and I'm waiting for the right time."

"And you intend to stay on my tail until then?" Tracker asked.

"Yep," Williams said again.

Tracker stared at the man, wondering how he could get him to change his mind without knocking him on his behind and getting himself arrested.

"All right," Tracker finally said, "just don't get in my way."

"I'll be behind you, Tracker," Williams said. "Just don't turn around too fast and I won't walk into you."

Tracker headed back to his hotel, planning his next move. He knew a little bit about Tom Howard now, and that was that nobody knew anything about him. Zee Howard was even more of a mystery to him. She seemed to be two different women.

It was time to look into the Ford boys a little.

In the hotel he approached the front desk and showed the old desk clerk a dollar.

"I'm plumb out of names, young fella," the man said regretfully.

"I need a place this time, Pop," Tracker said.

"What kind of place?"

"Where the Fords are staying. Are they from this town?"

"Nope. They come into town a little while before you did."

"Staying here?" Tracker asked, wondering if he could possibly get that lucky.

"Nope. They're staying in a small house on a hill just outside of town," the man answered. He pointed with a shaking hand and said, "North."

"Okay, Pop," Tracker said, dropping the dollar into the frail, outstretched hand. "Thanks."

"Any time, sonny."

Williams had not followed Tracker into his hotel, but had taken up a position across the street. Tracker left the hotel and, without more than a glance at the deputy, headed north.

St. Joe was not so large that you couldn't walk from one end of town to the other, so it wasn't long before Tracker reached the northern end of town. He kept walking beyond.

There were several houses north of town, but only one was on a hill. Tracker knew this was it. He started up the hill and took a short glance behind him to see if Williams was following. He was not. He had stopped at the edge of town and was leaning against a post, watching Tracker. As the house on the hill overlooked the town, it was very easy for Williams to keep Tracker in view as he approached the house.

Tracker mounted the rickety porch and knocked on the front door lightly. He was fearful that if he knocked any harder the door would simply fall off. The house was in desolate shape, and he found it surprising that anyone would choose to live there.

When there was no answer he risked a total collapse by striking the door harder. It quivered and rattled, but continued to stand. There was still no answer, and there were no telltale sounds from within. Tracker wondered if Dave Williams would take any kind of legal action if he forced the door and entered. Then again, the door wouldn't take much forcing, and from the vantage point of the deputy it might look as if the door had been unlocked.

Tracker decided to chance it. He braced himself and gave the door a push with his right hand. It popped open and he grabbed it to keep it from swinging freely. Without glancing down the hill to see what Williams was doing, Tracker entered.

The house was almost in as bad shape inside as it was out, but there were definite signs that someone was living there. There was not, however, anyone there at the moment. Tracker looked the place over briefly, but there was nothing there that could tell him anything about its occupants. He left, pulling the door shut behind him.

He had not yet stepped down off the porch when the first shot rang out and a bullet thudded into the side of the house inches from his head. He dove off the porch head first, avoiding a second, better-aimed bullet that struck the house exactly where he had been standing. He continued to roll, pulling his gun at the same time. He stopped rolling and came up on his knees with his gun at the ready, but there was nothing for him to shoot at. He waited patiently, his sharp eyes checking every possible place where a man could have fired from, but he saw no one, and there were no more shots.

Slowly, he rose to his feet and holstered his gun, then stood with his hands on his hips, still looking around. There were several—more than several— places from which those shots could have been fired, but there was apparently no one around anymore.

One place the shots might have been fired from was down the hill. From the sound of the shots, they would have been fired from a rifle, and that was an easy shot from the northern tip of town up the hill.

Tracker brushed himself off and started down the hill, but stopped short when he noticed something odd. His shadow was gone.

Dave Williams was nowhere to be seen.

[30]

Tracker went directly from the hill to the sheriff's office to find Dave Williams and ask him what he had seen. It wasn't normal for a deputy to witness a shooting and then just disappear.

He did not find Williams at the office, but he did find Jed Green, the sheriff.

"Sheriff," he said as he entered.

"Well, Mr. Tracker. What can I do for you?"

"You can tell me where your deputy is," Tracker suggested.

"My deputy. You mean, Dave Williams?"

"Who else would I mean? You got another deputy?"

"No, Dave's the only one. Don't need more than one in a town this—"

"Where is he?"

"What are you so all-fired upset about?" Green asked.

"He's been following me all day, Sheriff, whether on your orders or not, I don't know—"

"Dave's pretty much got a mind of his own," the sheriff said.

"Well, somebody just took two shots at me, and your deputy just watched and then disappeared. Now I want to talk to him."

"Hold on, Tracker," Green said. "Suppose you slow down and tell me exactly what the hell you're talking about."

Tracker explained, leaving out the part about forcing the front door of the house to get in.

"By the time I got to my feet, they were gone and so was your deputy," he finished.

"Well, maybe Dave just took off after whoever shot at you," Green suggested. "He's a go-getter, that boy."

"All right," Tracker admitted, "that's a possibility, but how about this one? How about if Dave was the one who took the shots at me?"

"Dave?" Green asked, surprised at the suggestion. "Why would he want to do that?"

"I don't know. That's one of the questions I want to ask him," Tracker explained. "How well do you know him?"

"Not all that well," the sheriff admitted.

"Is he from town?"

"No, he ain't. He come to town a couple of weeks ago. I needed a deputy and he needed a job."

"And that's all you know about him?"

"That's it, lock, stock, and barrel."

"And you gave him a badge?"

"Wasn't anybody else in this town willing to wear one," he explained. "I needed me a deputy."

"So he could be anybody," Tracker said. "He could be Dave Williams...he could even be Jesse James, for all you know!"

"Jesse James?" the sheriff said. "How could Dave be Jesse James?"

"Have you ever seen Jesse James?" Tracker asked.

"No, I ain't."

"Well, you got a woman in town who's his cousin. If we find Dave we can ask her."

"Jesse's cousin lives in town?" the sheriff asked, apparently unaware of that fact. "Who is he?"

"She," Tracker corrected. "Zee Howard says she's his cousin. You didn't know?"

"Zee Howard? Hell, Tracker, I don't know nothing about the Howards. They only been living in town a few months, and they pretty much keep to themselves."

"For a sheriff, you don't know much about what goes on in your town, do you?" Tracker asked.

Green stiffened and stood up.

"Now, lookee here, mister. I don't need no drifter

who sits in a saloon all day, drinking beer and playing cards, to tell me how to do my job. Now, if you got shot at, I'll look into it, and I'll ask Dave about it when I see him."

"I want to talk to him—"

"You ain't got no right to ask my deputy anything, mister," Green told him. "I'll check into the whole thing and let you know what I find out...as a courtesy, you understand, because you're a guest in this town." The sheriff stopped and squinted his eyes at Tracker, then asked, "By the way, just how long do you plan on being a guest of this town?"

"I haven't decided yet, Sheriff," Tracker said, moving for the door. "I haven't found what I'm looking for yet."

"And what's that?"

"You don't have the right to know that, Sheriff," Tracker told him. "I'll check on it and let you know...as a courtesy, of course, seeing as how I'm a guest in town, and all. Good day."

Tracker left the sheriff's office and headed for the saloon. He was angry, much angrier than he should have been, and he wanted a drink and a few moments to calm down.

He'd been away from this business too long.

[31]

"You did what?" Charley Ford asked his brother Bob.

Hesitant about repeating himself, Bob Ford said, "I took a couple of shots at that big stranger, Tracker."

"What the hell did you do that for?" his brother demanded.

"He was poking around our house," he explained, "and I thought maybe if he thought somebody was trying to kill him he'd leave town."

"Does he look like the kind of man who would run if somebody took a couple of shots at him?" Charley asked.

"No, but I figured it was worth a try," Bob answered. "And when I saw him in our house—"

"I guess there's no doubt that he was looking for us," Charley said. Shaking his head, he said, "I still don't think Jesse would send for someone to do his killing for him."

"I didn't believe it, either," Bob said, "but why else would this Tracker be looking for us? Who else could have sent him?"

"Maybe he's here on his own," Charley suggested.

"Why? I don't know him, you don't know him. What could we have done to him that he would be looking for us?"

"I don't know," Charley said. "Look, did anyone see you?"

"No, nobody saw me. I fired two quick shots and got out of there pronto."

"And you don't think you hit him?"

"I know I didn't hit him," Bob said. "Jesus, but he moved fast. I ain't never seen nobody move that fast—'specially not a man as big as him."

"Well, he ain't gonna run," Charley said, "I can tell you that. And now that somebody shot at him, and around our house, too—forget it. He ain't gonna stop until he finds us."

"We gotta kill him."

"We gotta kill Jesse, Bob," Charley reminded him, "and we can't do that if we're on the run from another killing."

"Nobody would have to know."

"If he's looking for us, and asking about us," Charley said, "and then he shows up dead, who do you think the law is gonna go looking for?"

Bob studied his brother's face for a few moments, then said, "Yeah, I guess you're right. What are we gonna do, Charley?"

"We just have to stay out of sight and wait until the time is right," Charley said. "We've got to keep our part of the bargain, so the governor will keep his."

They were in a cave about a mile out of town, which they intended to use in case something went wrong and they needed to hide from Jesse.

Nothing would go wrong, though. They would simply wait for the right time, and then they would kill Jesse James.

[32]

Tracker had a quick whiskey, and then a long, slow beer while he calmed himself down. When the beer was almost gone, he was back in control again. He still wanted to find the Fords—more than ever. He also wanted to find that deputy and have a long talk with him about how to do his job.

When he had mentioned to Sheriff Green that Dave Williams could be Jesse James, he'd only been trying to challenge the sheriff. Now he gave the possibility some serious consideration.

From what he knew, Jesse James was in his early thirties. His initial guess about Dave Williams was that he was in his late twenties, but yes, he could be in his early thirties. But would Jesse James be so foolish as to come to a town and take a job as a deputy? Or come to town with his wife and live under an assumed name? Wasn't that taking unnecessary risks?

More questions for Deputy Dave Williams, when he found him.

And for "Thomas Howard."

Tracker left the saloon and started making a slow circuit of the town, not asking any questions, but keeping his eye out for the Fords and for Deputy Williams.

At one point, while he was on one side of the street, he saw Zee Howard come out of the general store carrying a small package. He stopped to watch her. She

121

was wearing a high-necked dress that looked as if it were a size too large for her, but it couldn't hide the thrust of her large breasts. He tried to see in this woman the woman he had been in bed with last night, but couldn't. They were two totally different and separate women.

As if to bring that point home even more, she looked across the street right at him, yet failed to show any sign of recognition. She looked right through him, then set off down the street toward her house at a fast pace, as if afraid Tracker was going to follow her.

He did not. He didn't think he had to. Somehow, he felt that she was going to show up at his room again, that night. And then he realized that he would be disappointed if she didn't. He didn't delude himself that she was in love with him, or that he was in love with her, but being in bed with her had been an incredible experience. He didn't want it to become a once-in-a-lifetime thing, but— He also didn't need this kind of a problem when he was looking for Jesse James, especially if she was Jesse's cousin. He didn't intend to pursue her—as a woman, that is. If she chose to come to his room tonight, then fine. If she didn't—well, that would be just as well too.

He went through the entire town twice, and thought it odd that he didn't come up with either the Fords or the deputy.

Especially the deputy. He should have been around town, doing his job. Maybe Green had been wrong about him. Maybe he hadn't taken off after the shooting.

Maybe he had just been "taken" away.

As it was getting late, Tracker went over to the saloon to see if Jake Loomis and Wally Timms were there. Maybe Williams would be there too, or maybe one of his friends would know where he was.

When Tracker entered he saw Loomis and Timms sitting at the same table, but Williams wasn't with them. He went to the bar and got a beer, then went over to join them.

"Hiya, fellas," he said, sitting down.

"Hello, Tracker," Timms said.

Loomis just nodded and started dealing the cards.

"Whoa," Tracker said. "Aren't we a player short?"

"Uh—yeah," Loomis said, and continued to deal.

"Uh—Dave won't be playing tonight," Wally Timms said.

"Huh, why not? Tired of losing his money to me?"

"I guess he was just—uh—busy," Timms said, avoiding Tracker's eyes. "He's a deputy, you know."

"Yes, I know that," Tracker said. The cards were dealt, and as Timms reached to pick up his hand Tracker put one of his hands over the cards.

Timms looked at him, and Tracker said, "I want to know where Dave is, Wally."

"I don't know where he is, Tracker," Timms said. "Honest."

Tracker looked at Loomis, who jumped a little bit when the big man's eyes fell on him, and said, "Jesus, I don't know where he is. He's Wally's friend."

Timms threw Loomis a murderous look, and Loomis slid his chair back and said, "Uh—I gotta go. I'll see you fellas tomorrow."

When Loomis left, Timms said, "Well, I guess there's no game tonight, so I'll—"

Tracker moved his hand from Timms's cards to the man's arm, and he tightened his grip.

"How well do you know Williams, Wally?"

"I hardly know him at all," Timms insisted. "Don't listen to Loomis. He's just a drunk."

"Yeah, sure," Tracker said. He moved his hand and Timms started to push his chair back, but Tracker said, "Not yet, Wally. Have another drink with me first."

Tracker waved at the bartender, who brought Timms another drink.

"Tracker, what do you want from me?" Timms asked.

"Nothing, I don't want a thing from you. It's Dave Williams I want to talk to."

"Well, I told you, I don't know where Dave is."

"Yeah, I know you told me," Tracker said. He took a sip of his beer, then asked, "What do you know about the Ford brothers, Wally?"

"Who?"

"The Fords, Bob and Charley Ford. Do you know them?"

"I—uh—they may have come into my shop once or twice. Young guys, aren't they?"

"Yeah, they're both in their early twenties. Have they bought anything from you?"

"Uh—no, they haven't. They've come in once or twice, looked around, asked about a gun or two, and then left."

"Uh-huh, and that's the only contact you've had with them, right?"

"Right." Timms drank his whiskey and then said, "Can I go now, Tracker?"

"Sure, go ahead, Wally. You can go."

Timms pushed his chair back, stood up, and hurried out of the saloon like his tail was on fire.

Somehow, in a small town like St. Joseph, two brothers and a deputy had disappeared, and there was a possibility that Jesse James was there, too.

Somewhere...if he hadn't disappeared as well.

But if there was a possibility that he was in town, somewhere, there was also a possibility that he wasn't in town, had never been, and would never be in town.

That would mean that Tracker was on a wild-goose chase.

Still, Jesse and Frank could have been anywhere in the country. Missouri was just the best educated guess that law-enforcement officials and the Pinkertons could come up with...and Tracker had agreed.

He had to keep acting on that theory, or just give up.

[33]

Tracker went back to his hotel room that night to wait for Zee Howard.

That was not the way he consciously put it, but deep down, he was waiting for her to come again.

When the knock came on the door, he was cleaning his gun. He snapped the gun shut and carried it to the door with him.

"You must live a dangerous life," she said, looking at the gun as she walked in.

"Sometimes it's dangerous, yes," he said, closing the door. "Like the other day, with your husband. That was a potentially dangerous situation, all right."

She removed her wrap and said, "Oh, yes....Tom told me about that. I'm sorry."

"Did he also tell you what we discussed?" Tracker asked.

"He did. Did you know I would come tonight?" she asked.

He hesitated, then said, "Yes."

She smiled and said, "I guess you can see right through me, right? Were you hoping I would come?"

He didn't answer, and she said, "Yes, you were. You see? I can see right through you, too."

She walked up to him and put her hands on his chest, but as she began to unbutton his shirt, he grabbed her by the wrists and held her hands away from him.

"This isn't right, Zee," he said.

"What isn't right?" she asked. "What we had together last night? That isn't right?"

"That was wonderful," he said, "and it was exciting, but the reason for it wasn't right."

"Do I have to have a reason?" she asked, frowning.

"Yes, and a damned good one, too," he answered. "This woman, the one I was with last night and the one I'm looking at right now, is not you."

She looked down at herself and then back at him. "Who is it, then? Introduce me."

"I don't know who it is," he said, "but it's not the real Zee Howard."

She pulled her hands free from his grip and backed away from him. Her hands went to the buttons on her dress and undid them quickly. She dropped it to the floor, and hurriedly sent her underthings after it. Standing there gloriously nude, full breasts heaving with anger, or excitement—or both—she said, "This is the real Zee, Tracker. The one you want, and the one who wants you...now!"

Then she attacked him. That was the only way to put it. She pushed herself against him with full force, staggered him backward until his legs struck the edge of the bed, and he toppled onto it. She was crying, and cursing him through her tears. They both tore at his clothing. It wasn't easy with her on top of him, but with his help they got his clothes off, and then she slid down and took his rigid penis into her mouth.

"Christ!" he said through clenched teeth as she sucked on him furiously, as if she were dying of thirst and he was her only hope.

"Zee," he said, sliding his big hands under her arms and drawing her up.

"Shut up," she said, still sobbing. "Shut up, shut up." She pounded on his chest, then raised her hips and impaled herself on his shaft. He sank to the hilt in her and she began to ride him, biting her lips and moaning. This wasn't sex, he thought. It was some kind of punishment—but who was being punished? He reached up and grasped her large breasts, squeezed them together so he could suck both nipples simultaneously. At the same time, he began to drive himself up into her as hard as he could, and it became a contest of who could give the other the most painful pleasure.

When she came she pounded on his chest again, hard fast beats, like she was beating a tom-tom, and then he was emptying into her in almost painful spurts.

When they were finished she slid off him and sat on the end of the bed with her head bowed, bringing her sobs under control.

"That was a punishment for one of us," Tracker said. "And I think it was you. Why do you want to punish yourself, Zee? For having sex with me?"

"I don't know what you're talking about," she said.

"Get dressed," he told her, and proceeded to do so himself.

When they were dressed she walked to the window and looked outside, hugging her arms.

"Let's talk about your husband, and what he and I discussed."

"Let's talk about you and me," she shot back. "Forget about Jesse, Tracker, and I'll come to you every night, for as long as you want me."

"Forget about Jesse—" he said, and then stopped and took a long, hard look at her. "Is that what this was all about?" he asked then, incredulously. "You came to me last night, and now you're offering yourself to me in place of Jesse?"

She looked embarrassed and suddenly she was the same woman he had seen on the street, the same one he had seen in her house that first day.

"Zee," he said, walking up to her and putting his hands on her shoulders, "I don't want to hurt Jesse. I'm not out to catch him, or to kill him. I just want to talk to him. Tell him that."

He bent over, picked up her wrap and then put it around her shoulders.

"And you shouldn't have to trade yourself for any man, no matter how close he is to you. Not even if he was your husband."

She pulled the wrap around her suddenly, as if she felt a chill, and walked rapidly to the door. When she opened the door she turned around and looked at him again.

"I'll talk to Jesse," she promised, and left.

[34]

April 2, 1882

The next morning, after a night of nearly no sleep, Tracker was not very pleased with himself. Zee Howard, William Duncan, and everybody and everything that had had a hand in bringing him to St. Joe, Missouri, at this particular time. He realized that he had wanted Zee Howard to come to his room, and he was sorry that he had had to turn her away. He was not sorry that he *had* turned her away, only that he'd been forced to do so. He was also annoyed with her for trying to use her body to sway him from what he had to do. It had not been fair to either one of them.

Or to her husband, for that matter.

Tracker had breakfast, then made a halfhearted circuit of the town, looking for either of the Fords, and for Deputy Williams. He was not surprised when he failed to turn up any of them. He decided to put them aside—maybe for good—because if Zee could convince Jesse to talk to him, then it might be all over and he would not have to deal with anyone else.

He was still sorry that he had not been able to locate Frank, since that would have been the easiest way of all.

Then again, Tracker did not often find the easy way to do anything. The hard way always seemed more than able to find him.

The day he really started looking for the easy way

128

out was the day he would quit and go into the hotel business in San Francisco.

For good.

After having circled the town twice, Tracker decided to check with Sheriff Green, but he intended to keep his temper in check.

As he mounted the boardwalk to enter the sheriff's office, the door opened and Sheriff Green stepped out.

"Ah, Sheriff," he said, "you're just the man I was coming to see."

"If it's about that shooting, I haven't found out anything yet," he said.

"Did you check the bullets?"

"Mister, I couldn't tell which hole in that house had been made yesterday, or last year," he said.

Tracker thought back and remembered that the house had been pretty chewed up, at that.

"Have you found your deputy yet?" Tracker asked him.

"As a matter of fact, I haven't," Green answered, "and I don't mind telling you I'm pretty worried."

"I don't blame you. I'm a little worried, myself."

"You mean you don't think he's Jesse James anymore?" Green asked.

"I never did, Sheriff. I was just a little upset. You know how a man gets upset when somebody's been shooting at him."

"Sure. What do you think happened to him?"

"I'd like to find that out just as much as you do, Sheriff," Tracker told him.

"I'm shorthanded now, and if something should happen—"

"Listen, Sheriff. If something comes up and you need a hand, let me know. I'd be glad to give you a hand."

"If that offer is sincere, Tracker, I just might take you up on it."

"And if you should come across your deputy, just let him know that I'm interested in his welfare."

The sheriff studied Tracker for a few moments and said, "I'll get back to you, Tracker—if I locate him."

"I'm sure you will, Sheriff."

"Then again, if I find that you had something to do with his disappearance—"

"Sheriff, I'm the man who was shot at, remember?" Tracker reminded him.

"Yeah, so you say: All I know is, Dave was following you and now he's missing."

"Then you did order him to follow me."

Green shook his head and said, "I told you, Dave has a mind of his own. He told me that he planned to keep an eye on you, though, and I didn't think it was such a bad idea." He hesitated, then added, "Now I'm not so sure."

"I had nothing to do with his disappearance, Sheriff," Tracker assured him, "and I'm just as anxious to find him as you are."

"You just better hope he gets found, or I'm going to be looking for you."

"I won't be hard to find, Sheriff," Tracker said, "I won't be going anywhere for a while."

The sheriff stalked off and left Tracker wondering just where to go. There was nothing to do now but wait for Zee Howard to get back to him. She'd do one of three things: She would talk to Jesse and report that he said no to a meeting; she would talk to him and come back with a meeting place and time; or she would not talk to him at all because he was nowhere in the area, in which case Tracker would have to start looking all over again—or quit.

Tracker decided to do his waiting in the saloon, and if nothing happened by evening, he'd go looking for Zee and "Tom Howard" and see what he could do about forcing a meeting with the legendary Jesse James.

[35]

As darkness began to fall, Tracker finished his last beer and decided to visit the Howard house. It never occurred to him that he would not find them there, but that was the case. He knocked on the door, received no answer, knocked again, and then circled the house, peering in the windows.

There was no one inside.

Now he could believe one of two things. Either they had left town, or they were off meeting Jesse.

He checked around town and found that no buckboards, buggies, or horses had been removed from the livery by the Howards. Of course, they had their own horses, but could not have hoped to pile everything they owned on their backs. Neither had they purchased stage or train tickets.

Tracker decided to give them the night, and if nothing happened by morning...what? He'd have to make that decision when the time came. While there was still a chance that a meeting could be set up, he would have to just wait it out.

He stopped at the saloon for a bottle and took it up to his room with him. He halfway expected to find Zee Howard waiting there for him, but it was not to be. He went inside, opened the bottle, pulled a chair up to the window, and put his feet up. He wanted to take some time and *not* think, just drink.

He had lowered the level on the bottle to half when there was a knock on the door. Gun in hand, he answered. It was Zee Howard.

A little drunk, he asked her, "Have you come to offer me your body again?"

"No," she said, tightly. "I came to tell you to be at my house tomorrow morning, after breakfast."

He stared at her and then said, "Will he be there?"

She nodded and said, "Jesse will be there, Tracker. He'll listen to what you have to say."

"Thank you, Zee."

"Don't thank me," she said, "thank my husband...tomorrow, when you see him."

When she left, Tracker assumed his previous position by the window and thought about it. After a few more pulls on the bottle, he came to a decision.

It was too easy. Something had to be wrong because it was coming just too damn easy.

And what exactly did she mean by "thank my husband"?

[36]

April 3, 1882

The next morning Tracker could feel the tension crack-
ling in the air. Something had been building up since
the day he arrived—and even before—and today was
the day it would all come to a head.

He forced himself to have breakfast at a normal pace,
then surreptitiously checked his gun, out of sight beneath the table, before starting for the Howard house
and his meeting with Jesse James.

As he turned off the main street and started for Lafayette Street, a voice from behind him said, "That's
far enough, Tracker."

He stopped and tried to identify the voice. As he
started to turn he heard the hammer on a gun cock,
and the voice said, "There's no need to turn around.
Keep your hand away from your gun and walk to your
left. There's a small alleyway, see it? We're going in
there."

"For what?" Tracker asked.

"Just to wait, Tracker. That's all. Let's move."

Tracker recognized the voice now, as he started to
walk towards the alley.

It was the deputy, Dave Williams.

"What's it all about, Dave?" he asked. "You've been
missing for a couple of days."

"Uh-uh. Not missing. I knew where I was every minute," Williams informed him.

"Sure, but the rest of us didn't," Tracker replied. "We were worried about you."

"Sure you were."

"We didn't have a game without you."

"This is a different kind of game," Williams said.

They reached the alley and Tracker stopped.

"Keep walking, down the alley to the end—and don't think about running. This is the only way in or out."

"Nice choice," Tracker said, and continued on.

Tracker had no illusions about his ability with a gun. He was good, but he was not a fast-draw artist, and even if he was, he'd be foolish to try to draw on a man with a gun in his hands.

They got to the end of the alley, which had widened out into sort of a courtyard.

"Now I want your gun," William said.

"What's it about, Dave? What are we waiting here for?"

"You'll know soon enough. Take your gun out of your holster with two fingers of your left hand and drop it on the ground. Do it, Tracker. I don't want to kill you, but I will if you force me to."

"That's one choice I'd never force you to make, Dave," Tracker said. "If that's your real name."

"My real name doesn't matter."

"You know, for a while there," Tracker said, "I thought you might even be Jesse James."

Williams laughed and said, "Believe me, Tracker, this is the one day I'm glad I'm not."

The way he said it sent a chill up Tracker's spine, and now he thought he knew what they were waiting for.

"Come on, come on, the gun, Tracker," Williams prodded him. "Drop it on the ground and in a few minutes you'll walk out of here on your own two feet."

Tracker took the gun out of his holster, using just two fingers of the left hand, as instructed.

"Now drop it to the ground," Williams said.

"You sure you wouldn't rather have me toss it over to you?" Tracker asked.

"No—"

"Like that," Tracker added, and tossed the gun in a

134

lazy, high arc toward Williams. At the same time he launched himself at the man, aiming low.

Williams eyes went up to follow the arc of the gun, and before he could realize his mistake, Tracker hit him at the knees, knocking him over.

They scrambled around together in the dirt, both trying to gain a position of advantage. Tracker was not only trying to get on top, he was also trying to grab Williams's gun hand. To do so successfully, he had to give up the top position, so that while he had Williams's gun hand the other man was in the superior position.

Williams threw a punch that landed high on Tracker's forehead, and Tracker countered with a punch that caught Williams on his cheekbone. Neither blow, however, did anything to change their positions. They continued to struggle, Williams trying to free his gun hand from Tracker's grasp, but finding the bigger man too strong for him. In fact, it was Tracker's superior strength that eventually enabled him to reverse their positions. His left hand was still holding the "deputy's" right wrist, so he drew his right hand back and threw a punch that landed solidly on Williams's jaw. He felt the man go limp beneath him.

Barely giving the deputy a second look, Tracker retrieved his gun and ran from the alley, heading for the Howard house. He was almost to the door when he heard the shot, and knew he was too late. He knew that the shot meant the death of Jesse James.

Tracker paused momentarily at the sound of the shot, then accelerated and went right through the front door, almost snapping it from its hinges. His gun was held ready, but there was no need for it. All of the killing that would take place in that house had already been done.

On the floor in the living room Zee Howard sat, holding her husband's head in her lap. He was bleeding from a wound in his forehead.

Behind them on the wall a picture hung crookedly. A chair against the wall indicated that Howard might have been standing on it when he was shot.

The man who had shot him was still there. Tracker recognized him as one of the Ford brothers, although he did not know which one. Ford still held the gun in his hand, a silver-plated .44-caliber Colt that hung forgotten from his fingers.

Tracker walked to him and removed the gun from his hand.

"What happened?" he asked. "What the hell happened?"

"I killed him," Ford said. "I shot him. He climbed up on the chair to clean the dust off the picture—" The young man stopped short and gave Tracker a shocked look. "He didn't have his guns on. I never saw him without his guns on. It was my chance, my only chance."

"Your only chance?" Tracker asked. "For what? What did this man ever do to you?"

Tracker looked down at Zee Howard, who was trying to clean the blood from her husband's face. She looked up at him, her eyes filled with tears.

"He's dead," she said. "My husband's dead."

"Zee, I—" Tracker started, but her next words shocked him into total silence, although they didn't really come as a total surprise.

She said: "Jesse is dead."

Thomas Howard was Jesse James...and Jesse James was dead!

[37]

The immediate aftermath of the historic event was total confusion. Sheriff Green arrived on the scene and Tracker gave him Ford's gun. It turned out that Bob Ford was the one who had done the shooting.

Green's initial reaction was disbelief.

"That can't be Jesse James," he said, staring down at the body of "Thomas Howard."

"It is," Ford insisted. "It is. Ask her," he said, pointing to the woman known as "Zee Howard."

Green stepped forward, but Tracker put out an arm to stop him.

"Ask her later," he said, "Her husband's just been murdered."

"It wasn't murder," Ford insisted. "There's rewards out for him, dead or alive. It wasn't murder."

Tracker—the ex-bounty hunter—turned to Ford and said, "Shooting an unarmed man is murder, no matter how much of a reward there is on his head."

Ford lapsed into a confused silence, and Green instructed someone to go and get the undertaker. A crowd of people had pushed into the house, as the news that Jesse James had been killed traveled fast.

"Can't you get these people out of here, Sheriff?" Tracker said.

"Don't try to tell me how to do my job, Tracker,"

Green said. "I'll move these people out of here, all right, and I want you to move out with them."

Tracker didn't argue. He would have stayed if he thought it would help Zee, but her husband was dead and there was nothing that could help her now.

Tracker left the house in a daze. Jesse was dead, and he was too busy feeling sorry for Zee to worry about Duncan's watch.

Then he remembered Williams and rushed to the alley, but the man had regained consciousness and was gone.

Who the hell was he? He had obviously been aware that there was going to be an attempt on Jesse's life, and he had wanted to keep Tracker from interfering.

Why? Was he working with the Fords? And didn't this explain why the Fords had been so nervous and jumpy? They had been planning all along to kill Jesse, and were probably afraid of what he would do if he found out. It had probably been one of the Fords who had shot at him by their house, possibly because they thought he had been sent by Jesse to kill them.

Tracker left the alley where he had struggled with Williams and walked to the saloon. A few people who had seen him come from the Howard house stopped to ask him if it was true that Jesse James was dead, but he either brushed them off or ignored them.

Poor Zee. She had loved her husband enough to offer herself to Tracker if he would forget about finding Jesse. Had Jesse known about that? He didn't believe so. No husband would knowingly allow his wife to do something like that.

Tracker had a stiff drink in the saloon, then bought a beer and took it to a corner table. It was time for him to think about what this did to his job.

Jesse had finally decided to have a meeting with him, even though he had already spoken to him as "Thomas Howard." That must have meant that he agreed to at least listen to him. Had he guessed that the "item" in question was the watch?

And where was the watch? Was it on him? Would it now be buried with him? He hoped not. The watch meant a lot of money to him. He hadn't really thought much about the money, but it was too much to just forget

138

about. Half of it had been paid, and he didn't relish going back to San Francisco and paying that money back to William Duncan.

And on top of everything else, he wanted to find out why the watch meant so much to Duncan. In fact he had even considered not giving the watch back unless Duncan clued him in.

Maybe now that Jesse was dead, his brother's death would bring Frank James to town. Tracker could always work something out with Frank about the watch. Or with Zee, for that matter.

Tracker figured that now he would have a lot of waiting to do. It would be some time before he could approach Zee about such a thing.

He wondered what her plans would be now that Jesse was dead. Would she stay or would she leave?

And how long would he have to wait to find out?

[38]

April 4, 1882

The following morning Tracker went to the telegraph office to send two messages: one to Duke and one to William Duncan.

He told Duke that things were not going as well as planned, and then explained that he had found Jesse James, but that Jesse had been killed before he could talk to him.

His message to Duncan was a little more optimistic. He told him that he had found Jesse James and was making arrangements to retrieve the watch as soon as possible. He would notify him again when a price had been fixed, so that Duncan could wire him the money.

After sending the messages he went and had breakfast, after buying a copy of the town newspaper, *The Chronicle*. The front page headline was: JESSE JAMES KILLED IN ST. JOE! In smaller print it added: *Felled by an Assassin's Bullet!*

Tracker put the paper down on the table so that he could eat and still see the headline. His mind went back to a time six years ago when he had read about Wild Bill Hickok being killed in Deadwood, shot from behind by Jack McCall while playing cards.

Now here was another "legend" cut down from behind by a coward with a gun.

Ford had told his whole story to the newspaper. He had waited until Jesse had stepped up on a chair to clean off a picture, and just as he was about to fire, Jesse had turned around and looked at him, which was why he had been shot in the forehead.

As he had said to Tracker, he repeated that his chance had really come when Jesse had removed his guns. He quoted Jesse as having said that "It wouldn't do to have someone pass by and see me wearing all this iron. They might think there was a bad man in here."

Well, there had been, but his name wasn't Jesse James.

From the account in the paper, Bob Ford seemed to be very proud of what he had done, and he doubted that he would be prosecuted for "ridding the state of its worse enemy."

That quote did not sound like something young Bob Ford would say on his own. It sounded like something he'd heard someone else say at one time or another.

Somebody like a politician....

Tracker finished his breakfast, folded up the paper, and then walked over to the sheriff's office.

"What do you want, Tracker?" Green asked when he walked in.

"I saw Dave Williams yesterday," Tracker said. "I thought you'd like to know that."

"You saw Dave? Where?"

"I was on my way over to the Howard house to...to talk to them when he appeared, pulled a gun on me, and marched me into an alley...to wait."

"Wait for what?"

"I think he knew about this," Tracker said. "I think he knew that Ford was going to kill Jesse and he wanted to keep me from going to the house, for fear that I might stop it."

"Why would he do that?"

"Because he wasn't just Deputy Dave Williams, Sheriff," Tracker said. "In fact, I don't think that his name was Dave Williams at all."

"Then what was it?"

"I don't know, but I think he came here and got this job as deputy just so he could be around town. He knew there was some kind of a plot to kill Jesse James."

"That may be," Green said, "but I'd have to hear Dave's side of the story before I believe you."

"Sheriff, I don't think you'll hear from the man who called himself Dave Williams ever again."

"Okay, then," Green said, "suppose you tell me why you just happened to be on your way to that house on the morning that Jesse James was killed?"

"I was going there to meet with Jesse."

"You knew that Howard was Jesse?" he asked.

"No, I didn't *know* that, although it had occurred to me. Zee How—Zee James had told me that she was Jesse's cousin. She had arranged a meeting between me and him."

"What was this meeting about."

"I was hired to retrieve an item that Jesse stole during the Blue Cut train robbery. I was going to make him an offer to buy it back."

"What was the item?"

"It was a gold watch," Tracker said. "Sheriff, do you think I could get that watch—"

"Even if I believed you," Green interrupted, "I can't go giving you somebody else's property. Take that up with his family."

"Sure," Tracker said.

"Meanwhile, if I find out that you knew all along that Howard was Jesse James—"

"I already told you I didn't," Tracker said. "Has the body been positively identified yet?"

"His wife says it's Jesse," Green said. Then he made a face and said, "Timberlake is coming to town with a file on the James boys. He says there are certain scars and marks on the body that could make the identification positive."

"Timberlake is coming here?" Tracker asked. "What about Captain Craig?"

"Not that I know of," Green said. "Just Timberlake. He'll be here this afternoon."

"Where is Mrs. James?"

"As far as I know, she went back to her house."

"Have you got Ford in a cell?"

"I've got both of them in a cell."

"Both Fords? Why? When I got there Bob was the only one there."

"Well, he insists that his brother Charley was also in the room when he shot Jesse."

Tracker understood.

"He wants to make sure they both collect the reward," he said.

"That may be," Green said, "but I'm holding onto both of them anyway, until somebody tells me different."

"Like Timberlake? Or Craig? Or Crittenden?"

"Whoever," Green said. "One is as bad as the other, but you can be sure one of them will be taking over. I think they all deserve each other."

"Maybe," Tracker said, rubbing his jaw, "maybe so."

He was remembering how Timberlake did not want him to see the file on the Blue Cut job, and how if Timberlake didn't want him to see it, then that meant that Craig and Crittenden didn't want him to either.

He remembered how Bob Ford had called Jesse James "...the state's worse enemy."

"Can I talk to Ford?"

"No, you can't. You ain't family, and you ain't a lawman, so just get out of my office," Green said. "Or better yet, get the hell out of my town. The sooner I get you all out of my town, the better I'm gonna like it, I can tell you."

"Okay, Sheriff, okay," Tracker said. "I'll be leaving, probably tomorrow—after I talk to Zee James, and to Sheriff Timberlake."

"Just so long as you go," Green said.

Tracker left Green's office and stood on the boardwalk outside, thinking.

Something was fishy. He had a theory that had started when he read the quote attributed to Bob Ford. The Fords might have killed Jesse for the money, but the fact that he might have been Missouri's worst enemy would never have entered into it. That put together with Timberlake's efforts to keep him from reading the file and then coming to St. Joe convinced him that Timberlake was somehow involved in the whole mess.

In fact, he was more than sure that Timberlake had somehow put the Fords up to murdering Jesse James.

Now all he had to do was find some way to prove it.

[39]

Timberlake rode into town just after twelve noon. He felt elated that his plan had worked and they were finally rid of Jesse James. He was also glad that Tracker had not been able to ruin all of his plans.

His plan. He knew that Craig would try to take credit for it, but Crittenden knew the whole thing was Timberlake's idea.

Timberlake left his horse at the livery stable and walked over to the sheriff's office. He didn't relish talking with that idiot Green, but it had to be done.

The two men greeted each other coolly, and Timberlake said, "Do you have Ford in a cell?"

"I have them both in a cell, Sheriff Timberlake," Green said, "And they're all yours."

"I'd like to talk to them."

"Go ahead," Green said, picking up his hat. "I'm going out to get some fresh air."

The implication was not lost on Timberlake, but he let it pass. He had better things to do than match wits with Green. When Green was gone, Timberlake went into the back to talk to both of the Fords.

"Well, boys," he said, "it looks like things went along just as we expected."

"Timberlake!" Charley Ford said. "Listen, you've got to get us out of here."

"Now, now, take it easy, Charley," Timberlake said.

"You boys knew that you'd have to spend a little time in jail. That was all part of the plan."

"What about our reward?" Bob Ford asked. "Our ten thousand dollars."

"You'll be paid when the time is right," Timberlake promised. "Now let me ask you something. Are you sure he's dead?"

"He's dead, all right," Charley Ford said. "Bob shot him right through the forehead."

"With a forty-four," Bob chimed in. "A silver-plated forty-four that...that Jesse gave me as a present."

"Come on now, Bob," Timberlake said, "it's too late for second thoughts now."

"I know, I know," the young man said, "but you should have seen his face when he turned around. When he looked at me and knew what I was going to do." He turned to his brother and said, "He really had no idea that we were planning to kill him, Charley. He really trusted us."

"I know, Bob," his brother answered, "I know."

"Come on, boy," Timberlake said, "ten thousand dollars is ten thousand dollars."

He didn't want the Fords to start having doubts about what they had done. If that happened, they might talk, and that wouldn't work out for anybody.

"Look, just be patient," Timberlake told them, "I'll get you out of here as soon as I can. A little patience, and then you'll both have your money."

"We'd better get our money," Charley Ford said, "or everybody will find out exactly whose idea this all was."

Timberlake walked up to the bars until he was almost leaning on them and gave both of the Fords a hard look.

"I don't think you boys are in any position to be threatening anybody. Besides, who's going to believe a couple of backshooters over a lawman?"

The brothers exchanged glances as they realized how right he was.

"Just keep your part of the bargain," Timberlake went on, "and we'll keep ours."

Timberlake left them with that thought.

Bob and Charley Ford looked at each other, and both of them had some very heavy doubts on their minds.

"Charley," Bob said, "we'd better get that money."

"I know, I know," Charley responded, but both brothers were starting to wonder if they hadn't been set up just as Jesse was.

[40]

Tracker looked up from his table as Sheriff Green entered the saloon. The lawman walked to the bar and ordered a drink. Tracker picked up his beer and walked over to stand next to the sheriff.

"You're taking a pretty big chance, aren't you?" he asked.

"What do you mean?"

"I mean, leaving the Fords all alone like this. That is, unless your deputy has come back."

"No, Tracker, my deputy isn't back, but the Fords are not alone, either. Timberlake is with them."

"Timberlake is here?" Tracker asked with interest. "I guess he'll be staying at the hotel, then, won't he?"

"I don't know where he'll be staying," Green said. "Maybe in the stable with all the other horse's asses."

"Well, at least we share the same opinion of the man," Tracker said.

"Then maybe you're not all bad after all," Green said.

"I guess that remains to be seen, doesn't it?" Tracker said. He put his beer mug down on the bar and left, heading for the hotel. When he reached it, he saw Timberlake come out of the sheriff's office headed for the hotel. Tracker waited for him at the door.

"That's a little dangerous, don't you think?" Tracker asked him.

"Tracker!" Timberlake said. "I thought you went to Jefferson City."

"You were hoping I'd go to Jefferson City, you mean," Tracker said. "You were hoping I wouldn't get here in time to upset all your plans, right?"

"Plans?" Timberlake asked. "I don't know what you're talking about."

"Sure you do," Tracker said. "You sent the Fords after Jesse James, probably with the promise of some great reward."

"I don't have time to listen to your nonsense, Tracker," Timberlake said. "Let me by."

Tracker stood his ground and Timberlake bristled.

"Get out of my way, Tracker."

"I'm going to be in your way for a long time, Sheriff," Tracker said. "Until I can prove that it was you behind the murder of Jesse James."

"Murder?" Timberlake asked. "What murder? A dangerous criminal has been brought to justice by two good citizens. They are to be commended."

"And rewarded, right?" Tracker asked. "Isn't that part of the plan?" When Timberlake didn't answer, Tracker frowned and said, "Or is it."

"Let me by. I don't have any idea what you're talking about."

"You're going to let them hang, aren't you? You have no intention of giving them one penny of a reward. That was your plan all along, wasn't it?"

"I'll tell you the last time, Tracker. Get out of my way!" Timberlake said.

"I'll get out of your way now, Timberlake," Tracker said, stepping aside, "but it isn't going to be this easy to get me off your back. Count on it!"

[41]

To Tracker the inquest into the death of Jesse James was a thorough farce. Everyone who could possibly testify did—except himself. They even had Jesse James's mother up on the stand.

When Charley and Bob Ford testified, they made Jesse James look as bad as they possibly could, thereby making themselves look as good as possible. They testified that both of them had been there, but that Bob had been a little faster on the trigger and had shot first. They also said that they had killed him because Governor T. T. Crittenden had said he would like to see him captured, and because he had offered a ten-thousand-dollar reward for him.

Sheriff Timberlake and Captain Henry Craig both testifed that they had spoken to Robert Ford about *capturing* Jesse James, but that neither of the Ford brothers was directly employed by them.

The body of Jesse James was positively identified by scars and a birthmark that he was known to have. He was also identified by his wife and his mother. There was no longer any question but that the man who was killed, who had lived in St. Joseph, Missouri, under the name Thomas Howard, was in fact Jesse James.

The inquest was held on the fourth of April, and on the fifth the body was released to the family, who took it to Kearny, Missouri, the family's hometown, for burial.

Frank James never showed up—at least, not so that Tracker could recognize him.

Tracker was never able to get to Zee James to talk to her about the watch. Even if he had been able to reach her, he wasn't sure he would have been able to bring it up.

The more he thought about Dave Williams—or the man who had called himself Dave Williams—the more convinced he became that the man had been sent to St. Joe by Timberlake. That meant that the logical place to look for the man—and get him to admit that he worked for Timberlake—was Kansas City.

And that would be the first step to pinning a conspiracy charge on Timberlake and Police Commissioner Craig.

And, who knew...maybe on Governor T. T. Crittenden himself.

Tracker left for Kansas City at the same time that Zee James left for Kearny with her husband's body. Somehow he knew that they would both end up back in St. Joe sometime in the near future.

Part Four

[42]

Tracker arrived in Kansas City after dark. He put Two-Pair up in the livery and immediately went to the hotel to check in. After that, he had dinner in the hotel dining room.

When the waiter came to his table with his check, he also handed Tracker a note. It was from Mandy Locke. It said:

Please meet me in my part of town in an hour. MANDY.

Tracker paid his bill and tried to find the waiter who had given him the note, but the man had gone off duty. He didn't have time to try and locate him—especially if the man did not want to be located.

He knew that the note might be a phony, a trap, but he also knew that he owed it to Mandy to find out. He didn't know what might have happened to her after he left town. Timberlake might have suspected her of helping him, and he would not have taken that lightly.

Tracker decided to kill the remainder of the hour at the saloon.

The bartender remembered him and gave him a bartender's greeting.

"Hi, friend. Back in town again?"

"Passing through."

"What can I get you?"

"A beer."

Bringing the beer, the man asked, "Where you coming from?"

"St. Joe."

"Hey, really?" the man asked, leaning on the bar. "You were there when those dirty backshooters got Jesse?"

"I was in town, yeah."

"I hope they hang them up high, the dirty cowards," the bartender said with feeling.

"Did you know Jesse?" Tracker asked.

"I didn't have to know him. He was one of ours," the man answered. "Wait until his brother hears about this."

Tracker wondered about Frank, too. Where was he, and what would he do when he heard about his brother's death?

"Did Timberlake get back yet?" Tracker asked.

"Not that I know of. I'm sure if he had come back with them Fords the whole town would know about it."

"I guess so."

It was almost time for Tracker to meet Mandy, so he finished his beer and left the saloon.

Mandy's part of town was the southernmost part, and Tracker began to walk that way. He wondered why, if the message was really from Mandy, she had been so general about where to meet. Did she expect him to walk around until she approached him?

When he reached the less-desirable part of Kansas City, he had crossed what some towns call the "red line." Other towns simply called that part of town the "red zone." It was where the less-desirable whores had their cribs, and where the thieves in town were the safest.

It was also that part of town where the "honest" citizens were the least safe. As he crossed the invisible red line, he dropped his hand to his gun. He continued walking, hoping that Mandy would approach him before some sneak-thief did.

The further he walked, the more rundown the buildings became. Finally he came to a line of cribs, and the whores began trying to entice him in. There was nothing about any of these women, however, that he found the least bit enticing.

Until he came to the last crib. Here he thought that

he recognized the woman, and it took a few moments to finally realize that it was Mandy.

"Mandy?" he said.

She reached for him with dirty hands and pulled him inside.

"Tracker," she said, putting her arms around him.

She smelled of sweat and her hair was matted with dirt. She was not the same creature he had made love to only a week or so before.

"What happened?"

She released him and stepped back to sit down on the cot that was the only real piece of furniture in the room. The rest of the "furniture" was made up of cartons and boxes.

"Timberlake," she said finally. "He was sure that I had helped you that night, so he beat me up and had me sent here."

"Let me see your face, Mandy."

She lifted her chin so he could look at her in the dull light of her lamp. The change was shocking. Her eyes were red-rimmed and swollen, her bottom lip had been badly cut somehow, and had healed improperly. In addition to that, several of her teeth had been broken or knocked out.

She was no longer even remotely pretty, and he felt responsible.

"Mandy, I'm sorry," he said sincerely.

"Forget it," she said. "It's not important anymore. Listen, I saw you ride into town and I wanted to warn you. Timberlake was furious—"

"I've already seen Timberlake," he told her. "I can handle him, don't worry. When I got that note you sent me—"

"What note?" she asked. "I didn't send you a note."

"But you said you wanted to warn me."

"Yes. I was going to sneak up to your room later on tonight," she said, then lowered her head and said, "Although it wouldn't have been quite the same as last time."

He hardly heard her, though. The note had been a trap, and he had walked into it.

"Somebody sent me a note to come to this end of town."

155

"Then you've got to get out of here," she said. "Come on."

She went to the door to open it and check if it was safe for him to leave.

"Mandy, don't open the door!" he shouted, but he was too late.

As she swung the door open, several shots rang out, all of which smacked into her body audibly, flinging her backward.

They had expected him to be the first one out, and she had taken the bullets and saved his life, at the cost of her own.

Or whatever was left of it.

[43]

Tracker drew his gun and stepped over Mandy's body. He bent down to examine her and found that she was dead. He turned to face the door, but knew that he'd suffer the same fate if he tried to leave that way.

He looked around for another way out, but there was no back door. He touched the walls, testing them. The crib was made of the flimsiest kind of wood, and probably wouldn't have held up in a stiff wind.

If there wasn't a back door, he was going to have to make one.

He holstered his gun and lifted the cot off the floor. Holding it in front of him lengthwise, he ran at the back wall of the crib and slammed into it. His weight was too much for the wall, but instead of falling, as he'd intended, it simply splintered into pieces.

He stumbled as he drove through the wall and fell to his knees, throwing the cot to one side and drawing his gun. With the amount of noise he'd made, it wouldn't take them long to figure out what he had done.

He took off running behind the line of cribs, heading for a more well-lit part of town. He wanted to be able to see who he was shooting at. As he came out from behind the line of cribs, several more shots were fired, but they did not have much luck with a moving target. He kept running and then ducked into a darkened alley. He stopped just inside the mouth of the alley and flattened his back to the wall. He wanted to wait and see who was going to follow him.

He waited patiently, eyes open and ears alert, but after a few moments it became obvious that no one was going to follow him into that alley. The question was, had they given up, or were they waiting for him to come out?

He took some time to think over this most recent turn of events.

Timberlake was not yet back in town, but he could have figured out where Tracker was going when he left St. Joe and telegraphed ahead.

Could it be that Tracker had pushed Timberlake into a flagrant attempt on his life by telling him that he intended to expose his connection with the murder of Jesse James?

He hoped so. Maybe Timberlake had made a little mistake, and maybe in the very near future he would make a much bigger one.

Tracker finally decided to see if his would-be killers were waiting for him. He crouched down and peered around the corner and saw no one. He ran from the alley, his body tensed for the possible impact of lead, but there were no shots. Tracker kept on running until he crossed that intangible "red line" into the so-called "more civilized" part of town. Once there, he slowed down to a quick walk and kept as close to the buildings and as much in the darkness as was possible.

When he reached the busiest, most well-lit area of town—where the saloons were located—he holstered his gun.

He wasn't sure what to do at that moment about Mandy Locke's body, but he supposed that it wasn't going anywhere. In the morning he would go and see Timberlake, or maybe even Craig.

He wanted to make sure they knew that their men had failed, even though he had decided not to mention the incident.

And then, of course, he wanted to find the man he had known as Dave Williams—if Timberlake had not sent him into hiding.

Williams was the key by which he was going to bring the whole conspiracy down around Timberlake's ears.

Tracker stopped into the saloon for a drink, but stayed away from any conversation. After that he went to his room and spent the night in a chair with his gun in his hand.

[44]

April 6, 1882

In the morning Tracker discovered that Timberlake still had not returned, so he decided not to wait, but to go to the Muncipal Building and talk to the Police Commissioner, Captain Henry Craig.

Tracker was curious about Craig. He had already met Timberlake and he knew what kind of man he was. He was a take-charge man, and Tracker could not imagine him being subservient to anyone, not even a police commissioner or a governor. Now he was interested in seeing what kind of a man Captain Craig was, and he would do so by putting on a little pressure.

Tracker had to present himself to a secretary, a spinsterish woman who looked at him suspiciously when he asked to see Captain Craig.

"Do you have an appointment with the commissioner?" she asked.

"I don't, no," he admitted, "but I think if you tell him who it is, and that it concerns the Jesse James conspiracy, he'll be more than happy to see me."

She still looked dubious, but she said, "I'll check. Please wait here."

"I won't move a muscle," he promised.

She went into the commissioner's office and was there for only a few short moments before she reappeared.

"The commissioner will see you," she said, looking as if she couldn't understand why.

"Thank you."

She opened the door to allow him to pass through, then closed it behind him.

An unimpressive and obviously frightened man faced him.

"Mr. Tracker," he said, not bothering to rise, "I understood that you left Kansas City some time ago."

"Oh, I did," Tracker replied, taking a seat uninvited, "but I'm back now."

"May I ask why?"

"Sure you can."

Craig waited for Tracker to elaborate, and when it was obvious that he had no such intention, Craig said, "All right, then, why are you back?"

"I came back for Timberlake," Tracker said, "and anyone else who was involved in the conspiracy to murder Jesse James. Maybe that even includes you."

A muscle twitched in the man's face and he said, "I don't know what you're talking about. Jesse James was brought to justice by—"

"He was murdered, pure and simple," Tracker said.

"Even if that was true," Craig said, "why would you think that Timberlake, or I, would be involved."

"Because you didn't want me to see the file on the James Gang and the Blue Cut job, because that would lead me to St. Joe, and then I might get in the way. How high does this go, Captain Craig?"

"I still don't—"

"The governor?"

"The governor is an honorable man, Mr. Tracker," Craig said, becoming righteous. "He wants only what is for the good of the state. He wants to make Missouri a great state—"

"And Jesse James was in the way and had to be removed, right?"

"Mr. Tracker—"

"I wasn't at the inquest, Mr. Commissioner, but from what I understand, you admitted that the Fords were working for you—"

"Now, that's not so," Craig exploded. "We did talk to the Fords and we did mention something about capturing—*capturing*—Jesse James, not killing him."

161

"Either way it works out for you, though," Tracker pointed out. "Lucky, huh?"

He stood up.

"What is it you want, Tracker?" Craig asked.

"I told you. I want Timberlake, you, and anyone else involved with the cold-blooded murder of a man."

"Jesse James," Craig said. "A killer, for God's sake—"

"What are you sweating about, Commissioner?" Tracker asked. Craig's right hand flew to his forehead, feeling the wetness there. He swallowed convulsively, then looked at Tracker and said, "You don't know what you're doing. You don't know who you're dealing with here."

"Sure I do," Tracker said, walking to the door. "You just told me."

[45]

"He was here in my office!" Craig told Timberlake. "He could have killed me!"

"I should get that lucky," Timberlake said. "What did you tell him?"

"Tell him? I didn't tell him anything," Craig said, feeling the sweat pop out on his forehead again. He had never been so aware of how much he perspired until Tracker had brought it up.

"Come on, Craig. The man had you shitting in your pants, you must have told him something."

"I didn't tell him anything," Craig insisted. "I only warned him that he didn't know who he was dealing with."

"You what?" Timberlake said. "Don't you realize that if he suspected Crittenden of being involved, you confirmed it for him by telling him that."

"I didn't say anything—"

"Ah!" Timberlake said in disgust. "I'll have to send the governor a message. He's got to know that Tracker suspects him."

"You—uh—won't tell him—"

"I'll tell him everything he has to know," Timberlake said. "Now, what did Tracker say about last night?"

"Nothing, he didn't even mention it."

Timberlake tugged his mustache and said, "I don't understand that. He didn't say anything?"

163

"Nothing, I told you."

"Did you take care of the whore's body?"

"It was taken care of."

"What about Dave?" Dave "Williams" was actually Dave Wilson, and he worked for Timberlake.

"He wouldn't move until he talked to you," Craig said.

"What? You were supposed to get him out of town if he missed!" Timberlake reminded him.

"He's your man, Timberlake!" Craig shot back. "He wouldn't move until he talked to you!"

Craig had come halfway out of his seat and both men were facing each other across his desk.

"Sit down, Craig, before I knock you down," Timberlake said.

Craig hesitated and tried to hold Timberlake's eyes, but finally looked away and lowered himself into his seat.

"I'll talk to Dave, I'll send a message to the governor," Timberlake said. "You," he went on, pointing his index finger at the other man, "will not talk to anyone, and that means Tracker. Understand?"

Craig cleared his throat and said, "Uh—yeah, yeah, I understand."

Timberlake gave Craig a disgusted look and then left the office without another word. Craig put his head in both hands and stayed like that for a long time.

Outside, Tracker was waiting for Timberlake so he could follow him. He had been waiting for the sheriff to return, and when he did, two hours after his talk with Craig, he became his shadow.

Tracker assumed that "Dave" was at least one of the guns that had been shooting at him last night. Since he'd missed, Timberlake would probably want him to get out of town. A man like Dave wouldn't work for Craig, though, so he'd wait to hear from Timberlake.

Tracker hoped in fact—planned on it—that Timberlake would lead him to Dave.

Timberlake left Craig's office and started down the street. Tracker followed along, staying on the opposite side of the street, walking against the buildings so that the rest of the foot traffic would keep him hidden from sight.

When Timberlake cut down an alley, Tracker crossed the street quickly, not wanting to lose him. He looked into the alley, which had a dead end, but couldn't see anyone.

Timberlake had disappeared.

[46]

Tracker went back across the street and stepped into a dooway from where he could see the mouth of the alley. Timberlake went in, he was going to have to come out again.

Twenty minutes later Timberlake came out and headed in the direction of his office. Tracker waited until he was out of sight, then crossed the street again.

He walked into the alley, hoping to find a door, and didn't find it until he got all the way in. The dead-end portion of the alley was a boarded-up section that could be broken through easily enough, if the need arose. Right now, though, there were no loose boards that he could discern, so Timberlake had to have gone through the lone door.

Tracker faced the door and knocked on it.

"Who is it?" a voice called.

Tracker covered his mouth with his hand and called out, "I forgot something," hoping he sounded something like Timberlake.

He heard a bolt being thrown and then the door started to open.

"What did you for—" Dave was saying, but when Tracker's shoulder hit the door, the other man was cut off in midsentence, thrown back into the room.

Tracker rushed inside and shut the door behind him. Dave was on the floor against the wall, and when he

166

saw Tracker he tried to get to his feet, clawing for his gun. Tracker didn't want to have to kill him, so he took two steps and threw a kick that caught the man in the chest. Dave slumped to the floor and Tracker reached down and plucked his gun from his holster. He then reached down, grabbed the man by the shirt, and hauled him to his feet, pinning him to the wall.

"What's your name?" he asked.

The man made a few unsuccessful attempts at speaking and finally croaked, "Wilson, Dave Wilson."

"You work for Timberlake?"

When he didn't answer, Tracker put one hand against Wilson's throat and applied pressure. When his face started to turn blue, Tracker released the hold and asked him the same question.

"Timberlake," Wilson answered.

"You a deputy?"

"No."

"Then what?"

"I do odd jobs."

"Like trying to kill me last night?" Tracker asked. "Like killing an innocent woman instead?" The man didn't answer, and Tracker went on. "What were you supposed to do in St. Joe?"

He had to reapply the pressure to the man's throat before he finally answered.

"I was just supposed to make sure you didn't get in the way," he answered.

"Who took a shot at me at the Ford house?"

"One of them, I don't know which one."

"Where'd you go?"

"I tailed him to a cave outside of town. Part of my job also was knowing where they were at all times."

"What do you know about what was supposed to happen in St. Joe?" Tracker asked.

"Just that the Fords were supposed to kill Jesse James," Wilson answered.

"They made a deal, right? With Timberlake and Craig?"

"Yes."

"To kill Jesse, not just capture him."

"Look, Tracker, Timberlake will kill—"

"Mister, you won't walk out of this room alive if you

167

don't answer all of my questions," Tracker said. He was a few inches taller than Wilson and a lot stronger, so he literally lifted the man off his feet, holding him beneath the chin, just to illustrate his point.

"Understand?"

The man nodded as best he could, and Tracker lowered him to his feet.

"They were supposed to kill Jesse," Wilson said.

"For a reward."

"Right."

"Whose plan was it?"

"Timberlake's."

"And he cleared with Crittenden?" When Wilson didn't answer, Tracker slammed him against the wall and said, "Did Crittenden approve the plan?"

"Yes!"

"Okay," Tracker said. He released the man and stepped back. "We're going over to the newspaper office."

"What for?" Wilson asked, rubbing his throat.

"You're going to tell them the whole story, and they're going to print it."

"I can't," Wilson said. "Timberlake—"

"Once the story is in print, Timberlake won't touch you. He'll be too busy trying to save his own neck. Let's go."

Wilson picked up his hat and put it on, and preceded Tracker out the door. Tracker marched him to the newspaper office. At one point they passed Timberlake in the street.

"Jesus!" Wilson said.

"Keep walking," Tracker said. "He can't do a thing in front of all of these people."

That was the truth. The worst Timberlake could do was stare at both of them malevolently as they continued on to the newspaper office.

When they reached the office Tracker asked for the editor, who turned out to be a fairly young man of about thirty.

"What can I do for you?"

"I have a story for you, concerning the death of Jesse James," Tracker told him.

"Indeed? I'll run anything you have on Jesse as long

as it doesn't downgrade him. He was one of our own, you know."

"It's a shame that the governor did not share your opinion," Tracker told him.

"I beg your pardon?"

"Sit down, Dave," Tracker said, pushing the man into a chair, where he sat with shoulders slumped, looking miserable.

"This man's name is Dave Wilson," Tracker said. "He works for Sheriff Timberlake, and he has a very interesting story to tell you."

The editor looked at Wilson expectantly, and Tracker said, "Go ahead, Dave. Start talking."

[47]

The next morning Tracker walked into Timberlake's office and found the lawman reading the paper.

Timberlake looked up and saw Tracker and put the paper down.

"What do you expect this to accomplish?" he asked.

"Not much, I guess. Or maybe we won't know that until election time. We could have a new sheriff in Kansas City, a new police commissioner, maybe even a new governor in Missouri."

Timberlake laughed unconvincingly and said, "I doubt it."

"Well, I guess we'll just have to wait and see," Tracker said.

"You're really proud of yourself, aren't you?" Timberlake asked. "You really feel like you've accomplished something."

"I don't like murder, Timberlake," Tracker said. "The reasons for why I did what I did are as easy as that."

"Jesse James was a thief and a killer."

"He was also a man. Any man deserves to die facing his killer," he said, thinking of Hickok, and of Jesse James, and of himself.

"I hope you're not thinking about doing anything to Dave Wilson," Tracker said.

"That would be futile," the lawman replied. "Besides, Wilson has already left town. We can't undo what you've done, Tracker, we'll just have to see what kind of overall effect this—" he tapped the newspaper—"has."

"What kind of effect do you see it having?" Tracker asked.

"I don't know about the governor and Craig," Timberlake said. "They're more politicians than anything else, but me? I'm just a lawman doing my job."

Tracker saw what he meant. If anyone came out of this thing unscathed, it would probably be Timberlake. He was right, especially about Crittenden. The voters wouldn't have to believe what the papers said about their involvement with the killing of Jesse James. It would simply have to cross their minds just before they went to vote in the next election.

"I see your point."

"Does that bother you?" Timberlake asked.

"What?"

"The thought that I might come out unscratched?"

"I'm not thinking about it," Tracker said. "I did what I had to do. People know the truth now, so they can decide for themselves."

Tracker stood up and started for the door. When he reached it he opened it, then turned back to Timberlake.

"I'll be in San Francisco," he said.

Timberlake laughed again.

"I won't be coming after you, Tracker," he said. "That wouldn't accomplish anything, and besides, I won't have to." Timberlake tapped the top of his desk and added, "I'll be right here."

"Yeah," Tracker said, "I bet you will."

Tracker left the office and went to the hotel to settle his bill and get his things.

He intended to make one last stop in St. Joseph, and then from there it would be back to San Francisco, back to Deirdre, Shana, Will, Duke, the hotel . . . and back to Duncan, to find out just what the hell was so important about that watch, anyway.

[48]

T. T. Crittenden was, if nothing else, a realistic man.

He sat in his office in the governor's mansion in Jefferson City and knew it wouldn't be his much longer. What he did he honestly believed he had done for the benefit of Missouri, but the voters would never see it that way. They would always see him as a man who condoned the assassination of their hero, their Robin Hood, Jesse James.

His political career was ruined. Any hope he had of reaching the presidency was shattered.

When his term ran out, he would not be reelected, and there was nowhere else for him to go in politics.

He blamed Timberlake.

Henry Craig looked out his window from his office in the Municpial Building, and *he* knew that before long he'd be in the street, looking at the window from the other side. He would try to explain to the voters what had happened, that it was not his fault or his plan, but he knew they wouldn't listen. He only hoped that it wouldn't be Timberlake who would end up with his job.

He blamed the whole thing on Timberlake.

Timberlake was glad that he wasn't a politician. True, he would have to win an election to retain his job, but the voters would blame the governor and the police commissioner. Timberlake was just a hard-working sheriff doing his job. He knew that the original plan was his, but the voters would naturally blame the higher-ups for the idea. Timberlake's part in the execution of the plan was just that, his job.

The whole thing was a calculated risk, and he did not even hold it against Tracker for getting it into the papers.

Timberlake didn't blame anyone, because after all was said and done, he would still be sheriff, and Jesse James would still be dead.

Epilogue

[49]

Tracker returned to San Francisco without letting anyone know that he was coming. When he entered the
hotel, the first one he saw was Deirdre, who was man-
ning the desk.

"Can I have a room, please?" he asked her. She had
been looking down at some paperwork and answered
without raising her head.

"How long will you be staying, sir?"

"That depends on whether or not you'll visit my room
regularly," he said.

She looked up with a quick answer on her tongue,
but when she saw him her look turned to surprise.

"Tracker!"

"I'm back."

"You're back!" she said, as if she hadn't heard him.

"That's what I said."

"Why didn't you let us know?" she asked.

"Because I didn't want anyone to know," he said.
"I'm going upstairs. Will you find Duke and send him
up?"

"Sure," she said. "I'm glad to see you too."

He grinned at her and picked up his saddlebags.

"You can show me how glad later on, okay?"

"We'll see," she said.

"Sure. Tell Duke to bring up a bottle, too. Thanks."

He went up to his suite, which was one of the few

rooms in the hotel with a bath. He made use of it and then changed his clothes. He was feeling refreshed—but thirsty—when Duke finally arrived.

"Why didn't you let me know you were coming back?" Duke asked.

"I didn't want anyone to know," Tracker said, taking the bottle from him. "Drink?"

"Yes. Didn't you get my message?"

"What message?"

"I sent you a telegram in St. Joseph," Duke said, accepting his drink. "You didn't get it?"

"No, but don't be surprised. It was probably intercepted."

"Did you have trouble?"

"Yes."

"Were you involved with that shooting?"

"I was around, yeah."

"I read about Governor Crittenden condoning the murder," Duke said. "I guess he's washed up in politics."

"I guess so. What was the message you sent me?"

"I had some time on my hands," Duke said. Then he explained, "Uh—things were kind of slow."

"Go on."

"I checked him out, Tracker."

"What's his real name?"

"Oh, his real name is Duncan, all right. He was truthful in what he told you, as far as I can see. It's what he didn't tell you that I found so interesting."

"Which is?"

"He's a government man." When Tracker didn't answer right away, Duke said, "He works for the government, Tracker."

"I heard you."

Tracker poured himself another drink and thought it over.

"Of course, that doesn't mean that the government had anything to do with his hiring you."

"Keep quiet for a few minutes, will you, Duke?"

Duke lapsed into silence and watched his friend think. Finally, Tracker said, "What could be so goddamned important about a watch?"

"Maybe you should ask him. Did you get it?"

Tracker didn't answer.

"Is he staying at the same hotel?"

"Yeah, the Alhambra?"

"Has he been in here at all while I was gone?"

"Not exactly."

"What do you mean, not exactly?"

"He's had a man watching the hotel every day."

"The same man?"

"No. Three or four, rotating."

"Do they know you've spotted them?"

"No."

"Damn!" Tracker snapped. "He must know I'm back by now."

"So?"

"I want to know what's so important about a watch," Tracker said. "I want him to tell me, but I wanted to pick the time and place."

"Maybe he'll wait for you to contact him."

Tracker shook his head.

"If he's having the hotel watched, it's because he wants to know when I return." Tracker crossed the room and looked out the window. "I'll wait for him to make a move," he decided.

"If he comes, do you want me to send him up?"

"Send me a message. Tell Shana and Deirdre."

"Shana quit," Duke said.

"Tell Will to tell her I'm back," Tracker said, seemingly unconcerned. "She'll come back."

Shaking his head, Duke said, "You're so sure of yourself..."

"Don't start in with me now, Duke."

"Me?" Duke asked innocently. "Do I tell you how to treat your women?"

"Every chance you get," Tracker said, putting down his glass. "Look, go downstairs and see if one of his men is still watching the hotel. Then meet me in the dining room for dinner."

"Okay."

Duke got up, put down his glass, and left the room.

William Duncan was a government man. That put a whole different light on everything Tracker had gone through. He didn't for one moment believe there was any coincidence involved.

He had been used by Duncan, and maybe by the

179

government. Whether or not it all had anything to do with Jesse James he did not know for sure. All he knew for sure was that he had been used, and Duncan had engineered the whole thing.

Duncan would come looking for his "watch" sooner or later, and that was when Tracker would turn into the engineer.

He had been used, and he did not like it. He intended to find out exactly why.

When there was a knock on the door he knew it was too soon for Duke to have gone all the way downstairs and come back up. Deirdre was the only other one who knew he was back, so it wasn't hard to guess who was at the door.

When he opened it she smiled at him and said, "I missed you. Got a few minutes for a friend?"

"More than a few," he said. He put one arm around her waist and drew her into the room. He was already kissing her when he used his other hand to shut the door.

"Did you miss me?" she asked, putting her arms around his neck. "Oh, forget that," she added, quickly. "Even if you did you wouldn't tell me."

"I can show you," he said.

He picked her up as if she were a feather and carried her to the bed. She began to undress when he set her down, and was naked and ready for him when he lay down beside her.

After his experiences with Zee Howard James, Tracker found that he enjoyed sex with Deirdre that night more than any other, not because she was better that night—or because he was—but because it was sex without any ulterior motives.

"Oh, Tracker," she sighed as he began to nibble her breasts and nipples. "I hate myself for saying it, but I really missed you."

When they had first met, Deirdre tried her best to dislike Tracker, and even now her relationship with him was at least partially against her better judgment.

At that moment Tracker had feelings for Deirdre that he'd never had before—or had never admitted to. He cradled her in his arms and kissed her mouth, her eyes, her throat, her shoulders, her breasts. Releasing

180

her, he kissed his way down her body and then began to use his tongue to stimulate her.

"Oh, God," she said, touching the back of his head with her hands.

It was a bold move on Tracker's part. He'd done this sort of thing before with Shana, but not with Deirdre. His "partner" was not as inventive and free in bed as was the redhaired girl.

Deirdre, not quite sure about what she should do, entangled her fingers in his hair and just held on, moving her hips in time to the touch of his tongue. When she shuddered and came, he didn't give her a chance to relax. He moved up and entered her in one swift movement, and she gasped and wrapped her arms around him, holding him close.

"Hold me, hold me," she told him, meaning that she wanted him to cup her buttocks in his hands. She liked when he did that, when he took control—and she hated herself for that, too. Maybe that was why she was so stubborn and pigheaded when they were out of bed, because once they got into bed, she gave herself up to him in a way she could never do otherwise.

He cupped her buttocks and controlled the tempo of their movements, carefully building up to the moment when they would both come together.

As the moment approached she took his face in her hands so that she could kiss him, thrusting her tongue into his mouth. She surprised herself, never balking when he began to use his mouth on her, and also not hesitating to kiss him afterward. Had she missed him that much, that anything he wanted to do with her—or to her—was all right with her?

No, maybe it wasn't because she had missed him—although she certainly had. Maybe it was simply that she wanted him, needed him that badly.

Suddenly the pleasure of their mutual completion drove all thoughts from her mind, pleasure that was almost unbearable.

"God," she sighed, afterward. She turned her head to look at him lying next to her and said, "You were different, somehow."

"How?"

"I don't know...exactly, just different."

"Well," he said, sitting up. "Maybe I am different."

"How?"

He started to get dressed to go down to the dining room. She waited and watched him dress and then asked again, "How?"

Strapping on his gun he said, without looking at her, "Maybe I appreciate you more. I'll see you later."

"I'll wait here," she called out as he went out the door.

You bastard, she thought, you did miss me.

[50]

He was in the dining room when Duke came in.

"Have you ordered?" Duke asked.

"No," Tracker said. Duke was surprised that the big man had waited for him, but said nothing. They both ordered dinner and then Tracker asked him what he found outside.

"There's a man there, but it's a different one than was there this morning."

"Okay, then that means Duncan knows I'm back," Tracker said. "We'll wait for him."

The waiter brought their dinner, and while they ate, Tracker told Duke a little of what had happened.

"You mean you talked to Jesse without even knowing it?"

"Yes."

"And Frank wasn't around?"

"No."

"Jesse James," Duke said, shaking his head. "What was his wife like?"

"Why?" Tracker asked.

Duke shrugged and said, "Just curious."

Tracker examined his friend's face for a few moments, and was satisfied that it was indeed idle curiosity that had prompted the question.

What else could it have been?

"She was...pretty...loyal...and in the end, grief-struck."

"Did you see her after his death?"

"Briefly."

Tracker had told Duke nothing about Zee coming to his room those two nights.

Duke was about to speak again when he saw from Tracker's face that someone of interest must be approaching their table. He turned and saw two men, both well dressed, neither of whom was William Duncan.

"You know them?" Tracker asked.

"Yes," Duke said. "They've each taken their turn watching the hotel."

"Uh-huh. Our friend decided not to come himself."

The two men came up to the table and one of them addressed Tracker.

"Mr. Tracker?"

"Yes."

"I have a note for you, sir," the man said, handing Tracker an envelope.

Tracker took it, opened it, read it.

In a neat, precise handwriting, it told him that Duncan could not come for the watch himself, so he was to give it to these two men.

Tracker looked up at the man who had given him the note.

"I have your money," the man said. He patted his breast pocket.

Tracker put the note down on the table and said, "Give my friend the money."

The man smirked and said, "Give my friend the watch."

Tracker stared at the man and then looked at Duke.

"Duke, give the man the watch," he said.

Duke had known Tracker long enough to know that something was up when he asked him to give the man something that he did not have. Tracker obviously wanted him to give the man something that he did have.

Duke flicked his wrist and pointed a two-shot derringer at both of the men.

"Hey—" the delivery man said. When he looked at

184

Tracker, he found himself also looking down the barrel of Tracker's gun.

"Give my friend the money," Tracker said.

The man hesitated, but then removed a brown envelope from his breast pocket and handed it to Duke.

"Now, do you see this?" Tracker said, indicating his food with the barrel of his gun.

The man frowned but nodded jerkily.

"This is what's left of my dinner," Tracker said. "After this, I intend to have something for dessert. You tell Duncan that if he's not here before I'm finished with my dessert, I will consider our business finished."

"Do you have the watch?" the man asked.

"Just deliver the message."

"Aw, look, mister, if I don't bring that watch back and I come back without the money, Duncan is gonna give me hell."

Tracker cocked the hammer on his gun and said, "Friend, if you don't get your ass out of here and deliver my message, I'll send you to hell."

The man studied Tracker long enough to decide that he believed him, and he nudged his companion and they left.

"Here's your money," Duke said, handing Tracker the envelope. He tucked away his little gun and then looked at his friend.

"What's it all about, Tracker?"

"I don't know yet, but I intend to find out," Tracker replied. "I don't like being used. Why don't you finish your dinner and then go out front to wait for Mr. Duncan."

"Where will you be?"

"I'll be here, having dessert. Bring him in."

"What if he doesn't come?"

"He'll come," Tracker said, starting to eat again. "He'll come."

185

[51]

Tracker was almost finished with his pie and coffee when he saw Duncan enter the dining room, followed closely by Duke.

The government man did not look very happy.

He sat down opposite Tracker and demanded, "What's the meaning of this? Didn't you get my note?"

"Coffee?" Tracker asked.

Duke pulled out a chair and sat down.

"No damn it, I don't want any coffee," Duncan said. "Didn't you get my note?"

Tracker ate his last chunk of pie, chewing and swallowing very carefully.

"How was I supposed to know that you wrote the note?" he then asked.

"They had the money, didn't they?"

"That's right," Tracker said, "they *had* the money. I've got it now."

"Then I want what I paid for," Duncan said.

"I want something too," Tracker said.

"You have your money."

"I want more."

"More money?"

"No. I want some information. I want you to answer a few questions."

"What kind of questions?"

"Did you know about the plan to kill Jesse James?"

"Jesse James?" Duncan asked, frowning. "Is that what this is all about?"

"Did you?"

"I didn't know anything," Duncan said. "I read about that whole affair in the papers, Tracker. It was a co-incidence. Jesse James took that watch from me and I needed it back. That's the only connection I had with him, I swear."

Tracker studied the man and decided that he was not lying about that.

"Do you have it?" Duncan asked.

"Who do you work for, Duncan?"

"What?"

"I said, who do you work for?"

Duncan took his time deciding on what his answer would be, and then he decided on the truth—for once.

"Chester A. Arthur," he said, and Duke shot Tracker a quick look.

"The President of the United States?" Duke said.

"That's right."

Duke looked at Tracker again and said, "He's here, Tracker, in San Francisco."

Duncan nodded and said, "Yes, and he's come for that watch. I was on my way here with it when the train was held up."

"That was months ago," Tracker said.

"He thought he could do without it. When he decided that he couldn't, he asked me to try and get it back."

"Why you?" Tracker asked. "What do you do for him?"

"I'm the head of the Secret Service," Duncan said. He took out his wallet and showed Tracker his iden-tification.

"Jesus," Duke said, but Tracker wasn't impressed.

"With all the men that you've got, why pick me? Why spend the extra money?"

"My men tried, Tracker. They couldn't get near Jesse. I decided that the job needed a special man. I called Allan Pinkerton, and he recommended you."

"Now the big question," Tracker said. "Why didn't you just come right out and ask me? Why did you have to try and use me without telling me what it was all about?"

Duncan shrugged and said, "I thought that was the

best way to play it. Your reputation says that you work alone."

"You checked me out."

"Of course. I did a thorough background check on you."

"Did your background check tell you that I don't like to be used?" Tracker asked.

"Now, wait a minute, Tracker," Duncan said. "I can appreciate your being upset—"

"Upset?" Tracker asked. "You've got me wrong, Mr. Duncan. I'm not upset."

"Well, good. I knew you'd understand."

"What's in the watch?"

Duncan stopped and stared at Tracker.

"I can't tell you that."

"It's not the watch," Tracker said, "it's what's in the watch. It's got to be."

"You opened the watch?" Duncan asked, suddenly.

"Opened it?" Tracker asked. "I don't even have it, Duncan. I never got it. Jesse was killed before I could even talk to him about it."

"What?" Duncan said, paling visibly. "You don't have it?"

"No."

"But...you took the money."

"Yeah. I figure you owe it to me, anyway. For all the trouble I've been through, without knowing what it was all about."

"You can't—"

"Yes, I can."

"Tracker, the country needs that watch."

"Well, then, the country had better go and buy it. I hear they're holding an auction in St. Joe in a couple of days. They're going to sell everything that Jesse James owned at the time of his death. If you get there in time, you can probably get the watch cheap—on top of what you paid me, of course."

Duncan seemed at a loss for words, and Duke had his little derringer ready, just in case. There was no need, however. Duncan simply stood up and stared at Tracker.

"You haven't heard the last of this, Tracker."

"You better hurry," Tracker said. "The watch might go on the block first."

Duncan threw Tracker a murderous look, turned on his heel, and marched out.

"I think I'll have some more coffee," Tracker said.

"Tracker," Duke said with exasperation, "do you have the watch or not?"

"Do you know where the President is staying, Duke?"

"Yeah, sure. It's been in the papers."

Tracker reached into his pocket and came out with a large gold watch on a gold chain.

He dropped it on the table, right in the center, and said, "Take this and deliver it to the President, with my compliments."

Duke laughed and picked up the watch.

"You sent Duncan on a wild-goose chase," he said happily. He looked at the watch and asked, "Did you look inside? What's inside, Tracker?"

"It doesn't matter," Tracker said. "It doesn't matter at all."

Author's Note

On April 3, 1882, Jesse James was indeed shot by Robert Ford. That is historical fact. It is also fact that the plan for Robert and Charley Ford was conceived by Sheriff Jim Timberlake and condoned by Police Commissioner Captain Henry Craig and Governor T. T. Crittenden. When their part in the conspiracy became known, Craig and Crittenden were both ruined. Timberlake, however, retained his job, since he was looked upon as simply a lawman who was doing his job. All of the above people, and Zee James, are true historical characters. I do not claim, however, that the personalities shown in this story were their true personalities. I have no way of truly knowing what kind of people they were.

At the time of his death, Jesse James was living at 1318 Lafayette Street in St. Joseph, Missouri, under the name Thomas Howard.

TRACKER
TOM CUTTER

This adventure series features Abel Tracker, a 6'4",
cardplaying, hardfisted, womanizing, ex-bounty
hunter who is as handy with a gun as he is with
his fists.

THE WINNING HAND, Tracker #1
83899-0/$2.25
When Tracker becomes the owner of a San Francisco
hotel after winning a high-rolling poker game, he
finds himself caught up in a boxing match with
Kid Barrow and entangled with three pretty women
and two of the deadliest gunfighters in California.

LINCOLN COUNTY, Tracker #2
84152-2/$2.50
Tracker continues to brawl with the best gunfighters and indulge his appetites with the most
beautiful women in the West. In his latest adventure
bullets come after Tracker faster than women—when
he has to teach some manners to Billy the Kid.

AVON Paperback Originals